The strange

Murray Leinster

Alpha Editions

This edition published in 2024

ISBN : 9789362990976

Design and Setting By
Alpha Editions
www.alphaedis.com
Email - info@alphaedis.com

As per information held with us this book is in Public Domain.
This book is a reproduction of an important historical work. Alpha Editions uses the best technology to reproduce historical work in the same manner it was first published to preserve its original nature. Any marks or number seen are left intentionally to preserve its true form.

THE STRANGE PEOPLE
BY MURRAY LEINSTER
1

According to Cunningham's schedule there was a perfectly feasible route to romance and to high adventure. It began wherever you happened to be and led to Boston. There you took a train to Hatton Junction and changed to an accomodation train of one passenger coach and one baggage car. That led you to Bendale, New Hampshire, and there you hired a team. Both romance and adventure were to be found somewhere around Coulters, which was eight miles from Bendale. Cunningham was sure nobody else knew this secret because he had found it in a highly unlikely place and almost anybody else who happened to look there would find only dry statistics and descriptions.

However, as he boarded the accomodation train he inspected his fellow passengers carefully. One upon a quest like Cunningham's likes to feel that his secret is his alone.

At first glance the passenger coach was reassuring. There were a dozen or more passengers, but with two exceptions they were plainly people of the countryside. New England farmers. Two women who had been shopping at the Junction and were comparing their bargains. A swarthy French-Canadian mill-hand with his dark-eyed sweetheart. Odds and ends of humanity; the "characters" one finds in any New England village.

But even the two men Cunningham recognized as outsiders like himself were wholly unlikely to be upon the same quest. One had the solid, pleasant expression of a safe-and-sane man of business on his vacation, perhaps in search of a good fishing-stream. The other was a foreigner, immaculately dressed and with waxed mustaches, who was reading something that Cunningham could not see and exhibiting all the signs of mounting rage. Cunningham might have become curious about the foreigner at another time. He might have tried to guess at his race and wonder what reading-matter could fill any man with such evident fury.

But being upon the last stages of the route to romance, Cunningham thought of nothing else. As to whether the girl would be as attractive as her picture, he had no idea. Whether or not she had been married since it was taken, he could not tell. What reception he would receive at the end of his journey was highly problematical. He might be regarded as insane. He might—and he hugged the knowledge to him tightly—he might run a very excellent chance of being killed.

This was folly, of course, but Cunningham had an ample excuse. For ten years he had toiled at a desk. He had worn a green celluloid eye-shade and added up figures in a tall ledger, or made notes in a day-book, or duly pounded out, "Yours of the fifteenth instant received and in reply would state..." at the dictation of his employer. For eight hours out of the twenty-four, for eleven and a half months out of the twelve, he made memos or orders and payments and violations imposed and repairs made, and all connected with the business of a firm which installed and repaired elevators.

And now he was free. An uncle, dimly remembered, had died without any heirs but Cunningham. Cunningham had inherited fifty thousand dollars and within ten minutes after receiving the news had resigned his job and punched his employer's rather bulbous nose.

Now he was in quest of adventure and romance. He considered that he had earned them both. Ten years of law-abiding citizenship in New York entitled him to all of adventure he could gather, and ten years in a boarding-house earned him at least one authentic romance.

Cunningham had in his pocket the picture of a girl who lived a mile and a half from Coulters, New Hampshire. The picture had been taken four months before and her name was Maria. She was a pretty girl and had smiled at the camera without self-consciousness. That was all that Cunningham knew about her, but he had built up dreams to supply the rest. And he was quite insanely confident that where she was, there would be romance.

But romance alone would not do. There must be adventure as well. And adventure was duly promised. The picture was in the *Geographic Magazine* which travel- and adventure-hungry folk devour. It was one of the illustrations of an article prosaically entitled *Ethnological Studies in New Hampshire*, which very soberly outlined the radical traits of New Englanders and the immigrants who are supplanting them. And Maria was a Stranger—one of a group of people who were a mystery and an enigma to all those around them.

They were two hundred people of unknown origin who spoke English far purer than the New Hampshireites around them and avoided contact with their neighbors with a passionate sincerity. They could not be classified even by the expert on races of men who had written the article. They were not Americans or Anglo-Saxons. They were not any known people. But whatever they were, they were splendid specimens, and they were hated by their neighbors, and they kept strictly away from all contact with all other folk. The New Englanders charitably retailed rumors that more than one inquisitive visitor among them had mysteriously disappeared. Strangest of all, they had appeared from nowhere just two years before. They had bought ground and paid for it in new, rough gold. And they refused violently to give any account of themselves.

This was where Cunningham was going. Where the prettiest girl in the world had smiled unconsciously at a camera just four months before. Where a magnificent unknown race was represented in the hodgepodge of New England's later day. Where inquisitive strangers might mysteriously disappear, where certain hostility awaited too much questioning—and where the prettiest girl in the world might possibly be induced to smile.

Cunningham knew it was foolish, but he considered that he had earned the right to be a fool.

Then he looked up. The solid-looking man just opposite him had unfastened his suit-case and taken out a sheaf of magazine pages, neatly clipped together. He began to go through them as if they were totally familiar. Cunningham caught a glimpse of a picture among them, and started. It was the same article from the same magazine that had sent him here.

Then he heard a snarl, as of one who has contained himself until he can do so no longer. His head jerked around and he found himself staring at the foreigner who had seemed so angry. The man had the *Geographic Magazine* in his hand. It was open at the page—the very page—on which the girl was pictured. But the foreigner was looking at the type. Otherwise Cunningham as one in quest of romance and adventure would have felt it necessary to interfere an instant later. Because the foreigner glared at the page as if he had read something that infuriated him past all possible control and suddenly ripped the sheet across and across again, and threw the magazine upon the floor and stamped upon it in a frenzy of rage.

He saw eyes fixed upon him, some startled and some slyly amused. He sat down quivering with wrath and pretended to stare out of the window. But Cunningham saw that his hands were clenching and unclenching as if he imagined that he had something in his grasp which he would rend to bits.

2

The accommodation train made innumerable stops. It stopped at "South Upton." It puffed into motion and paused at "East Upton." A little later it drew up grandly at "Upton." Then it passed through "North Upton."

The comfortable-looking man opposite Cunningham looked across and smiled.

"Now, if we stop at West Upton," he suggested, "we can go on to a new name."

Cunningham nodded and on impulse pulled the *Geographic Magazine* out of his pocket and held it up.

"Same trail?" he asked.

The other man frowned and looked keenly at him. Then his face relaxed.

"I belong to the lodge," he admitted. "Here's my copy."

Cunningham jerked his head at the third man.

"He had one too. He just tore it up. It seemed to make him mad."

"That so?" The other looked steadily back at the foreign-seeming man, who was staring out of the window with his face pale with fury. "Let's ask him."

He caught the foreigner's eye an instant later and held up the magazine, opened at the article on the Strange People.

"How about it? You going there too?" he asked pleasantly.

The foreigner went purple with fury.

"No!" he gasped, half-strangled with his own wrath. "I do not know what you are talking about!"

He jerked himself around in his seat until they could see only his profile. But they could see his lips moving as if he were muttering savagely to himself.

"My name's Cunningham," said Cunningham. "I want to see those people. They sound sort of interesting."

"And my name's Gray," said the other, shifting to a seat beside Cunningham. "I'm interested, too. I want to hear them talk. Dialect, you know. It's my hobby."

"But they're supposed to talk perfectly good English——" began Cunningham, when he stopped short.

The train had halted leisurely at a tiny station and the conductor was gossiping with an ancient worthy on the station platform. A single passenger had boarded the coach and entered the door. He looked unmistakably unlike the other natives in the car, though he was dressed precisely in the fashion of the average New Englander. But as he came into full view at the end of the aisle he caught sight of the foreign passenger Cunningham had puzzled over.

The newcomer turned a sickly gray in color. He gave a gasp, and then a yell of fear. He turned and bolted from the train, while the foreign passenger started from his seat and with the expression of a devil raced after him. The newcomer darted into a clump of trees and brushwood and vanished. The well-dressed passenger stood quivering on the platform of the day-coach. The conductor gaped at him. The other passengers stared.

Then the well-dressed man came quietly back inside and to his seat. Veins were standing out on his forehead from fury and his hands were shaking with rage. He sat down and stared woodenly out of the window, holding himself still by a terrific effort of will.

Gray glanced sidewise at Cunningham.

"It looks," he observed in a low tone, "as if our trail will have some interesting developments. That man who just ran away was one of the Strange People. He looks like the pictures of them. It ought to be lively up in the hills when our friend yonder arrives. Eh?"

"I—I'll say so," said Cunningham joyously.

He talked jerkily with Gray as the train finished its journey. Without really realizing it, he told Gray nearly everything connected with his journey and his quest. Cunningham was busily weaving wild theories to account for the scene when the first of the Strange People appeared before the third passenger. Otherwise he might have recognized the fact that Gray was very cleverly pumping him of everything he knew. But that did not occur to him until later.

Gray looked more at ease when the train reached Bendale and he and Cunningham sought a hotel together. They saw the third man sending a telegram and, again, arranging for a horse and buggy at a livery stable. He ignored them, but his lips were pressed together in thin, cruel lines.

Cunningham was very well satisfied as he arranged for his room and for a team to take him to Coulters the next day. Ostensibly he was going to try for some fishing, though nothing larger than minnows would be found in that section. But Cunningham considered that the route to romance and adventure was beginning to offer promise.

Still, next morning both he and Gray were startled when the hotel-keeper came to them agitatedly.

"There was three strangers on the train yesterday, wa'n't there?" he asked in a high-pitched voice that trembled with excitement.

"Yes," said Cunningham. "Why?"

"D'ye know the other man?" asked the hotelkeeper excitedly. "Know who he was or anything?"

"No, not at all," Cunningham answered alertly, while Gray listened.

"Would ye recognize him if ye saw him?" quavered the hotel-keeper.

"Of course," said Cunningham. "Why? What's the matter?"

Gray had struck a match to light a cigar, but it burned his fingers as he listened.

"He rented a horse an' buggy last night," quavered the native. "He drove off to Coulters way, he said. An' this mornin' the horse came back with him in the buggy, but he was dead."

"Dead!" Cunningham jumped and found himself growing a trifle pale.

"Yes, dead, that's what he is!" said the innkeeper shrilly. "Them Strange People done it! Because it looks like he was beat to death with clubs an' maybe fifty men was on the job!"

3

The route to romance led through Bendale to Coulters, but now there was a dead man in the way. It had taken youth and hope and several other things to set out as Cunningham had done in the first place. The quest of a pictured smile among a strange people in unfamiliar country is not a thing the average young man can bring himself to. He will be afraid of looking foolish. But to continue on the quest when one has just seen a dead man the girl's own people have killed, more courage still is needed.

Cunningham was not quite so joyous now. He had gone with Gray to identify the foreigner. He had turned sick at the expression on the man's face. He had promised to stay within call for the inquest. And then he and Gray had gone on to Coulters.

Cunningham was not happy. Here was adventure, but it was stark and depressing. And romance. The pictured face was no less appealing and no less ideal. But the picture had been taken four months before. In the interval what might not have happened? Many people were concerned in the killing of the foreigner. Did the girl of the photograph know of it? Was she in the secret of the death that had been dealt out? Did she know who had killed the man, or why?

"You'd a lot better have stayed behind, Cunningham," said Gray, as their team jogged over the country road to the summer boarding-house where they were to stay. "I don't think this is going to be pleasant from now on. No place for a romance-hunter."

"You're not staying back," Cunningham observed. "And you're just following a hobby."

"Umph. That dialect business. Yes," said Gray. His lips twitched grimly. "But a hobby can be as exacting as a profession. Still, I didn't expect to come up here and run slap into a first-class murder."

Gray puffed on his cigar and slapped the horses with the reins.

"The pleasantest part," he added, "is that we shall probably be just about as unwelcome as that chap was last night."

Cunningham did not answer, and they drove in silence for a long time.

Discomforting thoughts assailed Cunningham. He knew as clearly as anyone that it was absurd to grow romantic about a girl merely from a picture. But though it may be absurd, it is by no means uncommon. The obtaining of autographed photographs from Hollywood ranks with radio as a national occupation. Cunningham was not disturbed by the comparative idiocy of traveling several hundred miles and running into some danger just to see a girl whose picture haunted his dreams. But the thought of finding her involved in such an unpleasant mess as the killing of the foreigner; that was different.

A tidy-minded person would have abandoned the quest at once. He would have abandoned the clearly marked trail to romance and high adventure and gone home. A man who acted upon sober common sense would have done the same thing. But such persons do not ever find romance and very rarely even the mildest of adventures. It takes folly and belief to come at romance!—such folly as enabled Cunningham presently to see his duty clear before him.

Maria needed someone to protect her. She was a Stranger, and the native New Hampshireites hated the Strange People cordially. Cunningham had heard enough at the police station that morning to know that the investigation of the foreigner's killing would be close to a persecution. But if Cunningham were there, near enough to protect the girl who had smiled so shyly yet so pleasantly at the camera, why——

Gray grunted suddenly.

"There's our boarding-house," he said, pointing with the whip. "I suppose the Strange People live up in the hills yonder."

Cunningham stared up at green-clad giants that were tumbled here and there and everywhere in inextricable confusion and grandeur. Hill and valley, vale and mountain, reared up or dipped down until it seemed that as far as the eye could reach the earth had once been a playground of Titans.

A four-square, angular building of typical New England build lay beside the road at the foot of the hills.

"They came here," grunted Gray, waving his whip. "They had gold, rough gold, to buy ground with. Where did they come from and why did they pick out this part of the world to settle in? The soil's too thin to grow anything much but hay. The ground's so rough you have to sow your fields with a shotgun. The biggest crops are stones and summer boarders."

"I'm wondering," said Cunningham, whose thoughts had wandered as his eyes roved the heights, "I'm wondering were they knew that chap that was killed."

"Where they knew him?"

"The Stranger on the train recognized him at first glance. But that chap had a copy of the *Geographic Magazine* and he'd found where they were from that. He had learned about them just as we did."

Gray frowned. Then he looked respectfully at Cunningham.

"You're right. They knew him somewhere, a couple of years ago. But where?"

Cunningham shrugged.

"The article says nowhere."

And the article did. According to the writer, the Strange People were an enigma, an anomaly, and a mystery. And they had just proved that they could be a threat as well.

The livery team drew up before Coulters' solitary building. It was a crossroads post-office and summer hotel with a dreary general store tucked under one wing.

A man was sitting on the porch, smoking. He was watching them intently and as they alighted he rose to greet them.

One glance made Cunningham exclaim under his breath. This man was the counterpart of the foreigner on the train—the one who had been killed. The same olive skin, the same keen and venomous eyes, and even the same too-full lips with their incongruous suggestion of cruelty. He was dressed, too, in the same immaculate fashion from meticulously tailored clothes to handmade boots.

"How do you do?" he said politely. "I've been hoping to find you here. You reached Bendale on yesterday's train?"

Gray's face was quite impassive.

"Yes," he admitted.

The foreigner exhibited half a dozen magazine pages. They were the ones containing the article on the Strange People which had brought both Gray and Cunningham to the spot.

"I believe you recognize this?"

Gray nodded, watching the man keenly.

"Before you arrange for rooms," suggested the foreigner, smiling so that his teeth showed unpleasantly, "I would like to speak to you a moment. My brother saw you on the train. He telegraphed for me to meet you here. I may add that I had myself driven all night over very bad roads to get here, and I probably ruined a car in trying to meet you."

"Well?" asked Gray shortly.

The foreigner reached into his pocket and pulled out a thick wallet. He opened it, and an incredible mass of yellow-backed bills was exposed to view.

"In the first place," he said pleasantly, "I would like to offer each of you a present—let us say, five thousand dollars apiece—just to go home and forget that you ever saw that magazine article or ever heard of the Strange People in the hills up there."

4

Gray turned to the buckboard and began to hand down his suitcases. The last of them was on the ground before he spoke.

"I'm afraid we can't do business," he said without expression. "I am here on a matter of scientific interest. I want to study their dialect. By the way, have you had any news from Bendale this morning?"

The foreigner shook his head impatiently.

"News? No. But if I make it ten thousand——"

"I'm afraid not," said Gray pleasantly. "I'm not in a money-making business. My friend Cunningham may be willing to take you up."

But Cunningham tossed his own suit-cases down.

"No," he said contentedly. "I came here for fun. For adventure, if you choose to put it that way. And anything I'm offered so much to stay out of must be too much fun to miss."

The foreigner gnawed at his fingertips as they started for the hotel.

"Wait a moment," he said urgently. "Perhaps we can still come to some agreement. You wish to study dialect? You wish to find adventure? We may still work together."

"How?" Gray put down his suitcases to light a cigar, while he gazed abstractedly at the foreign-looking man.

"I—I—er—my name is Vladimir," said the foreigner nervously. "I will promise you five thousand dollars each and all assistance in your separate desires. You"—he spoke to Gray—"you will have all opportunities to hear them talk and study their speech. And you, er, you shall have all the adventures the hills afford. If only you will, er, help us to maintain a certain, er, discretion."

Cunningham found himself disliking this man extremely.

"Discretion?" he demanded. "You mean keep our mouths shut?"

Vladimir beamed at him.

"Ah, yes! You are a young man. Adventure? There are pretty girls in the hills. I will give them orders. You will find them fascinating. And five thousand dollars in addition to smiles——"

"Suppose you talk plainly," said Gray shortly, before Cunningham could speak.

"You will find my brother among the Strangers," Vladimir told them eagerly. "You saw him on the train. Find him and tell him of the bargain I have just made with you. And he will tell you just what you may repeat or speak of what you see. And if you agree to work with us I will give you more money. Ten thousand dollars!"

"But what is the work you are planning?" asked Gray, again before Cunningham could reply. Cunningham was seething.

"It would not be wise to say. But the sheriff of the county has agreed to work with us—for a gift, of course—and will assist us with the full force of the law. If he does so, there can be no objection to your aiding us."

"Oh," said Gray gently. "The sheriff's in it too?"

"To be sure. He—he will guide you to my brother," offered Vladimir eagerly. "Do not go inside the hotel. Let the sheriff take you to the hotel where my brother waits. Talk to my brother. And you will earn ten thousand dollars each!"

Cunningham's head began to whirl. Vladimir hadn't heard of the death of his brother. But he had some plan to the detriment of the Strange People, and so obviously of Maria. Otherwise he would not have found it necessary to bribe the sheriff. And yet, both Vladimir and his brother had been at a long distance the day before. They had hurried here on learning where the Strange People were. The Strange People knew them and feared them; might even be hiding especially from them! But why?

Cunningham could not explain it, but he knew that he had not mistaken the route to adventure. Coulters was on the way. But there was a mile and a half still to go.

Gray moved suddenly.

"Cunningham, if you want to take up this proposition—"

Cunningham picked up his bags and moved toward the hotel.

"I can't fill the contract," he said shortly.

"But it is so simple!" protested Vladimir. "Simply talk to my brother—"

Gray was already up on the porch.

"Can't do even that," he said grimly. "You evidently haven't heard. You'd better get Bendale on the 'phone and find out. Your brother was on the train with us yesterday, it's true. He went up to the village of the Strangers last night. But his horse brought his body back this morning. They'd killed him."

Vladimir gasped, and went ashen. Sheer incredulity flashed across his features. Then he believed and was stunned. But there was no grief whatever to be seen on his face. Instead there was a terrible wrath, a rage so beastly and cruel that Cunningham shivered when he saw it.

"They killed him, eh?" he said very softly, like a cat purring. "They dared to kill him, eh? Ah, when I am through with them they will go down on their knees and beg me to kill them! Beg me!"

His eyes were fixed and glassy with fury. Cunningham instinctively looked for the foam of madness to appear upon his lips. But he turned and went softly within the hotel.

"Charming example of family affection," said Gray. "Why didn't you take his money?"

"I wouldn't miss this," Cunningham told him, "for ten times five thousand. What in blazes is up in those hills?"

"I suggest," Gray said dryly, "that we go and see. Got a gun?"

Cunningham nodded.

"There's no time like the present," grunted Gray. "The sheriff was over here, busily being bribed, when that killing was discovered. Let's get up in the hills before it's overrun with deputies. It won't take a second to get our rooms."

As a matter of fact it was nearly an hour later when they strode out of the hotel and made abruptly for the mountain-slope.

For another hour they scrambled up stiff slopes among thorny brushwood and small trees. Cunningham was already trying to sort out the hodgepodge of events. Adventure—or mystery at any rate—crowded about him. Romance must inevitably follow. That seemed so certain that he was almost able to discount it. He was sure by now that Gray was not in the hills for any study of dialects, and he contentedly ran over the list to date. A killing and the offer of a bribe. A corrupted sheriff and the threat of 'unspeakable revenge. And Gray——

Cunningham, you see, was following a definite route which cut across common sense and sanity. Therefore he kept his eyes open more widely than Gray. And therefore he was tingling all over with a not altogether pleasant thrill when Gray turned on him suddenly.

"Cunningham," he said sharply, "tell me the truth for once. Why did you come up here? Who sent you?"

Cunningham grinned, casting little side-glances at the trees about him.

"Nobody," he said joyously. "I came up here for adventure and for romance. And I'm finding them. For instance, there are half a dozen people hiding behind those trees and watching us."

"The devil!" Gray stopped short and stared about him. It was a creepy feeling to realize that they were being spied upon from the woods. Suddenly he saw a furtive movement as a blurred figure slipped from behind one trunk to another. Its figure was that of a man, but he could see nothing else about it. "Creepy, eh?" said Gray grimly.

"There's a girl with them," Cunningham told him. "*The* girl. Maria."

But Gray rushed suddenly at a clump of brushwood as if to seize something hiding there. A human figure started up and plunged away. And then something came flicking through the air, glittering, and stuck fast in a tree-trunk with a dull "*ping!*" It was a long-bladed knife, and it had missed Gray's throat by inches.

And without a word or a sign the air seemed suddenly full of the little flickering flames which were knife-blades glittering in the sunlight. And which, also, were death.

5

Cunningham flung himself down on the ground. His revolver came out instinctively, but he shouted, "We're friends, you idiots! Friends!"

There was no answer, but the knives stopped their silent rush through the air. It seemed as if the hidden men in the forest were debating in whispers, and the stillness was deadly. Cunningham lay still, gradually worming his revolver around to a convenient position for firing. He was tingling all over, but he found himself thinking with a supreme irrelevance that he thought he had seen the girl whose picture crackled in his breast pocket as he moved. He was quite sure of it.

He stood up suddenly and began to dust himself off. It was taking a chance, but it was wise. A young man stepped out from among the trees near by.

"You are our friends?" the young man demanded skeptically. "We have no friends."

His speech had but the faintest of slurs in it, a teasing soft unfamiliarity which pricked one's curiosity but could never be identified in any one syllable, much less put down in print.

Cunningham felt an abrupt relief, and quite as abruptly wanted to swear. He knew that this was the end of the route to romance and that the girl, Maria, was peering out from the tangled underbrush. And he had dived head foremost into a patch of loam and looked most unromantic. Therefore he said wrathfully, "If we weren't your friends, don't you think we'd have plugged into you with our gats? We saw you. You know that!"

The young man stared at him and Cunningham tried to rub the dirt off his nose and look dignified at the same time, thinking of the girl behind the trees.

Then the young man said skeptically, "What is a gat?"

"A revolver. A pistol. A handgun," snapped Cunningham. "We'd have wiped out the lot of you."

The man searched his face unbelievingly. A murmur came from somewhere behind him.

"Show me," he said. He came boldly out from the brushwood and faced Cunningham squarely.

He was no older than Cunningham, but Cunningham instantly envied him his build. He was magnificently made and splendidly muscled—as were all the Strangers, as Cunningham learned later. He met Cunningham's eyes frankly, yet defiantly.

Cunningham turned to where Gray still lay sprawled out in a heap of brush. Imperturbable puffs of smoke rose in the still woodland air.

"Go ahead and charm them, Cunningham," said Gray's voice dryly. "I'm under cover and I'll start shooting if they start anything."

"Show me that you could have killed us," repeated the young man, facing Cunningham. "Use this thing you have."

Cunningham held out his revolver. The Stranger looked at it curiously but impassively. He seemed totally unfamiliar with its nature or use.

"Great guns!" demanded Cunningham in exasperation. "Don't you know what it is?"

The young man hesitated and then shook his head.

"No. I do not know what it is."

He waited defiantly as Cunningham gaped at him. People in these United States who had never seen a revolver! He grunted.

"All right, I'll show you, then."

He picked up a bit of weather-rotted rock and set it up for a target. He drew off ten paces and leveled his pistol. He fired, and half the rock flew to fragments. It was seamed and cracked by the freezings and thawings of many years.

The young man flinched at the sound.

"It is like a shotgun," he observed calmly. "You can use it twice. And then?"

He tapped the hilt of his knife suggestively.

"Then this," snapped Cunningham.

He fired again and again and again. The rock was splinters.

"And I've still two shots left," he observed grimly. "My friend yonder has six more. If we were not your friends would we have waited for you to chuck rocks at us?"

The young man debated. He inspected Cunningham's face again.

"N-no," he admitted. "Perhaps not. But why did you come here?"

Cunningham reached into his pocket and flipped the torn-out pages of the magazine article to him.

"Look at the pictures. That's why I came," he said grimly. "And if you want to know more——"

The young man had cried out in astonishment. He turned and beckoned to the woods behind him. A second man appeared. Then a third. They stared at the pictures, fumbling them with their fingers.

The young man turned once more to Cunningham with a very pale face.

"Tell us," he begged. "How did these come to be? Tell us! If you are our friends, tell us everything!"

For all his blank astonishment, Cunningham realized that he had made a bull's-eye.

For ten minutes he talked to them, at first in commonplace speech, and as he realized that the most ordinary of technical terms meant nothing to them, he spoke as if to children. He watched their faces and explained until he saw comprehension dawn. And he became filled with a vast incredulity. These people spoke grammatical English, better than the native New Englanders. But they knew nothing of revolvers, though they had seen shotguns and rifles. They knew nothing of cameras, though they could read and write. And they were in a civilized state of a civilized nation! Only the most passionately preserved isolation and an incredible ignorance to begin with could account for it.

They listened intently. Now and again another figure crept out of the wood. They were sitting in a semicircle about him now, watching his face as he spoke. Old men, young men, but no sign of the girl. Presently the younger men began to comment to one another on what Cunningham was saying. Gray got up and sat down more comfortably with his back against a boulder. The comments of the younger men were low-voiced, and sometimes one or another of them smiled. Presently a little chuckle ran about the circle.

Cunningham stammered. He felt like a fool, explaining that he was here because of an article in a magazine, and then having to explain what a magazine was, what a camera was, and all the rest. It was when the feeling of folly was strongest upon him that the chuckle went around. And then he noted that the young men had been quietly retrieving the knives they had sent flickering through the air. Everyone now had his knife back in his belt and was fingering its hilt while he gazed smilingly at Cunningham.

The smiles were bland and friendly, but a feeling of horror came to him. They were playing with him! They were pretending to listen to him, but actually they were toying with him as a cat toys with a mouse. They ringed him about, now, thirty or more of them. From time to time they edged closer to him. And one of them would ask a question in that teasing soft unfamiliar dialect of theirs, which you could not put your finger on. And he would edge a little closer, and smile.

Sweat came out on Cunningham's forehead. He felt as if he were in a nightmare. The smiles were terrifying. They masked a sinister purpose, a deadly and unspeakable purpose. Cunningham was remembering the dead man he had seen that morning. Some of these men had done him to death. Now they were edging closer to him, feigning to listen and feigning to smile.

He turned and found half a dozen of them very close to his back. He whirled back again and saw that they had edged closer while his back was turned. They sat upon the ground with their eyes fixed intently upon him, and smiled when he looked at them, and asked questions in their soft and unfamiliar accent. And always they moved closer....

Cunningham felt that his teeth would begin to chatter in an instant. And suddenly a look of intelligence passed from one to another. A signal!

6

Cunningham suddenly swung his pistol out. He was sweating in the horror they had inspired. Once they came for him he would be calm enough, but this ghoulish waiting until he should be momentarily off his guard was ghastly. He flung out his pistol in a wide arc.

"I'll show you some target practise," he said suddenly. "Clear a lane over there."

He waved his hand and they parted reluctantly. Now and then they exchanged glances. He could see some of them peering about, as if looking to make sure that no one else was within sight. Cunningham managed to snatch a glance at Gray. Gray was staring at him with a queer distaste, and Cunningham tried to explain what he planned with a significant look. He'd clear a path for a rush, and then they could stand these people off.

He slipped fresh shells in place of the exploded ones.

"Now I'll hit that tree-trunk over there," he said sharply. Gray should understand and be ready to leap up. "Watch the bark fly."

But Gray was sitting quite still. He was regarding Cunningham suspiciously.

"Like this," snapped Cunningham. He glanced at Gray and made an almost imperceptible motion for him to jump up. They'd have to run for it in a moment.

He pressed on the trigger, and his eyes came back to the sights just as the hammer was falling. It was too late to stop the explosion and his heart stood still. From behind the very tree-trunk he was aiming at a girl's face had peered.

From sheer instinct he jerked at the weapon almost before his brain had registered his impression. It went off with a roar, and as the echoes died away he heard the rattling of several twigs falling to the ground.

Cunningham gasped and the revolver nearly fell from his hands as he saw her still standing there, gazing interestedly at him. He rushed toward her, his terror of an instant before all forgotten.

"I might have killed you!" he gasped. "Are you hurt? Are you?"

Her eyes opened wide and she flushed faintly. She moved as if to flee. Then she glanced at the Strangers grouped about the place Cunningham had left and stepped out into the open.

"You—you made a very loud noise," she said uncertainly. "That was all."

It was the Girl. It was Maria, whose picture Cunningham had treasured and about whom he had day-dreamed. At another time he might have risen to the high heroic moment. He might have appeared in better guise. But in the transcendent relief of finding her safe his wrought-up emotions found escape in the form of rage. He whirled on the Strangers.

"Why didn't you tell me she was there?" he demanded furiously. His horror of a moment before had vanished completely. He was angry enough to have waded into the bunch bare-handed. "You knew she was there! Damn it, I might have killed her! I might have shot her! Idiots!" he cried, half sobbing from relief; "you let me come close to killing her!"

Gray was still staring at him curiously.

"If you really mean these people well, Cunningham——" he was beginning curtly, when Cunningham turned to the girl again.

"Please forgive me," he begged, still white and shaking from his scare. "I didn't know you were there!"

Her eyes met his wonderingly. Then the expression in them changed. She read the terror and understood its cause. She smiled shyly.

"I was safe. My friends were there."

She meant the thirty or more Strangers, staring puzzledly at Cunningham and bewildered by his evident horror. Cunningham's head cleared with a jerk. He felt more than ever like a fool. All men are tempted to feel that way in the presence of a pretty girl, if only to keep the pretty girl company, but Cunningham saw that the Strangers were honestly at a loss. There had been no secret purpose. They were as incredibly uninformed as they had seemed and they had been listening with all the attention their actions had displayed.

"Look here," said Cunningham abjectly, "I guess I seem like a fool to you, Maria, but I did come here only to see you. I—I've been day-dreaming about you. Let me show you why I was scared and you'll understand what it would have meant if I had hit you."

He took her hand and fitted it to the pistol-grip. He put her finger on the trigger.

"Now, point it off that way," he went on anxiously, "squeeze on this thing...."

There was the swift thudding of horses' hoofs. A nasal voice cried shrilly, "Halt in th' name of th' law!"

Cunningham started and instinctively held fast to his revolver, which someone seemed trying to jerk away. He caught a glimpse of flying figures melting into the woods. Then he saw two men on horseback plunging up to the spot. One wore a bright star on his chest and the other carried a rifle.

"There, naow!" the sheriff of the county exclaimed, panting. "I got one of 'em, even if it was a girl."

He lunged from his horse and seized Maria, who was wrenching frantically to get her finger out of the trigger-guard Cunningham had held tightly.

She flashed a glance of bitter hatred at Cunningham.

"Easy," said Cunningham with sudden heat. "What are you arresting her for? I was showing her how to shoot a revolver."

"No thanks to ye for that, then," panted the sheriff. "Here, Joel, come an' help me get the cuffs on her."

Cunningham brought down a heavy hand on the sheriff's arm.

"What's this for?" he demanded hotly. "I didn't hold her for you!"

"I'm arrestin' her for murder, that's what. She's one of them Strange People, she is. An' they killed that furriner last night. You know that. You saw him this mornin'. Mr. Vladimir told me. Joel, come here an' help me. Help me get her hands in these cuffs."

Cunningham wrenched the sheriff's hands free.

"Don't be a fool," he snapped angrily. "That killing was the work of men! This girl had nothing to do with it!"

"I warn ye not to interfere with the law!" growled the sheriff.

"I'm not interfering with the law," said Cunningham hotly. "I'm interfering with your doing what Vladimir's bribed you to do! This girl would never get to jail. Vladimir's much too anxious to get some of the Strangers in his hands. Hands off!"

He thrust the girl behind him, where she cowered for a moment.

"Get out of here," snapped Cunningham. "And you start something about my resisting the law and I'll start something about your taking bribes! Clear out and leave this girl alone!"

"Ye better not shield a murderer——" whined the sheriff uneasily.

"If you want murderers, look for men," said Cunningham coldly. "Then I won't stop you. But stick to the law, Sheriff, and forget about Vladimir."

He drew back with the girl behind him and his eyes blazing. The revolver that had snared the girl was still clutched in his hand. The sheriff gazed at him venomously.

"I'll tend to ye," he said uncertainly.

"Try it," Cunningham growled as he watched the two men ride slowly away. He watched until they had disappeared. Then he turned to Maria.

She was gone.

Cunningham stared blankly, then grinned sheepishly at Gray.

"I guess that was foolish, maybe," he apologized, "but he made me mad."

Gray was white as a sheet, but he tried to smile as he got up stiffly.

"You did good work for me," he said grimly. "Look at my coat."

He turned and showed a little rip in the back.

"When those chaps made for the woods," he said grimly, "one of them dropped behind my own particular boulder and stuck the point of a knife in my back. If the sheriff had taken that girl off, the knife would have been sunk in me. Ugh! Let's go back to Coulters."

7

The hills rose until they blotted out half the stars, and the moonlight on their tree-clad slopes was like a screen of opaque lace against the sky. Utter solitude seemed to surround the little summer boardinghouse. No other house was in view. No lights burned in the houses the Strange People must occupy in the hills. All was silence.

Gray stood up and tossed away his last cigar.

"I'm going to turn in," he said at last. "It's too much for me. By the way, I may be gone before you get up in the morning."

"Leaving?" asked Cunningham.

He and Gray had been talking fruitlessly, trying to piece together what they knew of Vladimir with what they had seen of the Strangers, and attempting to figure out the connection between the two. They had decided that the Strangers' attack upon them had been due to Gray's rush at one of the hidden figures. That their hiding was due to the fact that they had killed Vladimir's brother and were afraid of arrest. But they could concoct no theory as to why Vladimir had sought them out, or where he could have known them, or why he was willing to spend any amount of money to have a free hand with them. Certainly they could not understand what he would gain besides revenge, or even how he could set about taking that in a civilized country.

"No, not leaving," said Gray. He yawned. "You don't care to confide in me, Cunningham? About your real reason for being here?"

Cunningham grinned. The route he had followed had not misled him. Adventure and romance were certainly about him. He had seen Maria, and she was perfect. And there was promise of more excitement.

"I've told you," he said cheerfully. "I came here for fun. Why not tell me why you came?"

Gray smiled.

"Dialect, of course." His tone admitted that he did not expect Cunningham to believe it. "I'll send some wires and be back by noon. Watch your step while I'm gone. I think Vladimir would feel happier with you in jail."

"I know he would," said Cunningham. "But there's something crooked going on. I shall object pretty strenuously to being arrested."

Gray laughed.

"I think you will," he admitted. "But today I thought you were just trying to hold the Strangers in talk until the sheriff could reach them unheard. I think they thought the same."

"I didn't hear the son-of-a-gun," said Cunningham.

Gray yawned again on his way to the door.

"I knew it when you fought to keep that girl from being arrested. Didn't you notice I told you about the knife at my back right away? So that the Strangers would hear me? I wanted them to know you'd kept her free on your own hook, not to save my life. That ought to make them believe in you somewhat."

"But why did you want to make me solid with them?" demanded Cunningham.

"Oh, you might help me later," said Gray dryly, "in studying their dialect."

He disappeared, and Cunningham frowned out at the darkness for a long time. It was a puzzling mix-up, and it might prove a dangerous one. Gray had been close to death that afternoon and one man had been killed. But Cunningham could not find it in his heart to dwell upon anything, now, but Maria. She was—different. Cunningham dwelt upon her image in his memory with increasing contentment. Sometimes a man sees a woman and without even any feeling of surprise realizes that it is she whom he has been waiting for all his life. It is more of a recognition than a meeting. Cunningham felt that way about Maria.

But he forced his brain to a last effort to understand the mystery into which he had dropped. Vladimir offering bribes to keep other people from the Strangers he hated, and the Strangers with their incredible lack of knowledge of American commonplaces.

"Vladimir's crazy, or I'm crazy, and maybe all of us are crazy," he muttered as he tossed his cigarette over the porch railing. "I'm going to bed."

He went up the stairs by the light of the turned-down lamp in the hall and fumbled with his key in the lock. He opened his door and struck a match. Then he uttered an angry exclamation.

A moment later he had lighted his lamp and was searching among his tumbled-about possessions for a sign of theft.

Someone had entered his room and searched his suit-cases thoroughly. His clothes had been ransacked. A bundle of letters and papers had been read and strewn on the floor. It looked as if every seam of his garments had been searched for hidden clues to his identity or motive in visiting Coulters and the Strange People.

Nothing was missing, but everything had been examined. Cunningham felt his anger mounting. Vladimir, of course. Why didn't the man want him there? What was he suspected of?

There was a gentle tapping at his window and Cunningham looked up with an increase of savagery. But—two faces were looking in at him. One was Maria, smiling a little. The other was a Stranger of middle age or over.

She put her finger to her lips and motioned for him to lift the window. Cunningham strode over and thrust it up. It was latched from the inside and the necessity of unfastening it dispelled a flash of suspicion that had come to him.

"This is my father, Stephan," whispered Maria. "We must talk to you."

The older man slipped into the room and after an instant's hesitation held out his hand. He looked weary and worn.

"I could not come any other way," he said slowly, picking his words with a trace of difficulty. "I would have had to kill the sheriff. But I wished to thank you, for Maria."

She had slipped in behind him and sat down on a chair. Stephan waited until Cunningham motioned him to another. There he sat quietly, fingering the hilt of his knife and looking at Cunningham with grave and not unfriendly eyes.

Cunningham was hopelessly at sea, but he felt a little tingling feeling of comfort. He looked at Maria, and there was an infinite deal of satisfaction in the glance. It was as if he saw her and knew with perfect certitude that some day she must love him. For himself, with sublime confidence he knew that his dreams were justified. It was insane, perhaps, but such things do happen. One worships very many girls, very earnestly, and then quite suddenly one glimpses another girl and—well, one *knows*.

Stephan's voice broke the silence again.

"I came," he said heavily, "to thank you for keeping Maria from being taken away. And I ask you if you are our friend, as you said. And why you came here."

Cunningham pondered the reply he should make. He saw Maria looking at him with a curious expression of dawning recognition, of surprized intentness. He glanced up and she flushed slightly. Very abruptly he saw that she had read his expression and that she was discovering the same odd certitude. Their eyes met for the fraction of a second. And then—it was as if there were no more need to speak. She flushed a vivid red, and after that her eyes had difficulty in meeting his.

That, also, was insanity. But such things happen likewise.

"I am your friend," said Cunningham gruffly, "if Vladimir isn't. I dislike that man."

His heart was pounding loudly, though no word had passed between Maria and himself. Stephan eyed him steadily.

"But I'm getting tired," added Cunningham, "of explaining why I came here and where I came from. Nobody believes me. But you didn't come to ask me those things only."

"No," said Stephan harassedly. "We came to ask you what to do."

"About what?"

"All things," said Stephan fiercely. "A man was killed. You know that. There is another man here. You call him Vladimir, and he will have to be killed also. And the sheriff comes and tries to take us away. What shall we do?"

Cunningham had trouble in thinking of an answer. He wanted to talk to Maria. He wanted to take her to one side and say innumerable things.

"About the first man," he said at random, "you ought to get a lawyer to advise you. And keep out of the way of Vladimir and the sheriff until he can tell you what you ought to do."

Stephan's face mirrored a resolute despair.

"No. We will not do that. He would ask who we were and why we killed that other man."

"He might," agreed Cunningham lightheartedly. He wanted desperately to talk to Maria. "People do that sort of thing around here."

Stephan looked at his daughter questioningly. She nodded, with shining eyes that evaded Cunningham's. Stephan tugged at his belt and placed something on the floor before him. He unknotted a string about a coarse cloth bag and poured out upon the floor a shining heap of gold-pieces. But they were not like any gold-pieces Cunningham had ever seen before. They were hammered from nuggets or bars by hand. They were square, about the size of a double-eagle and twice as thick, and still showed the marks of the hammer that had formed them.

"We will give you these," he said quietly, "if you will get us gats like the one you showed my people today."

"Gats? Oh ... guns. Pistols."

Stephan nodded and swept the gold-pieces into a shining array. The sight of them sobered Cunningham abruptly.

"But what will you do with them?" he asked. "How will you use them? What do you want them for?"

Stephan spread out his hands.

"Then we will not need a lawyer," he said grimly. Cunningham caught his meaning.

"How many people do you chaps plan to kill with them?"

Stephan smiled sadly.

"Not many. Only until we are left alone."

"You people do need a guardian," growled Cunningham. Maria was watching him with soft eyes that always just evaded meeting his. Cunningham felt that a tremendous responsibility was being thrust upon him. "Look here——"

There was a sharp knock at the door.

Cunningham hurled himself at the doorway to bar entrance until Stephan and Maria should have time to get away. All the Strangers were considered outlawed now. Cunningham had only their safety in mind, but Stephan misread his swiftness of movement. With lightninglike quickness he was on his feet with bared knife, darting likewise to the doorway.

Cunningham's hand came down with a jerk. The knife flew from Stephan's hand and stuck quivering in the floor. The next second Cunningham's revolver was out.

"Steady!" he whispered sharply. "Steady!"

Then Maria had flung herself in front of the revolver. All this was done in fractions of seconds and almost without sound.

"You shall not let him be taken!" she whispered fiercely. "You shall not!"

Stephan's whole frame was alert and his eyes were flaming as if he were sure this was a trap and waited but the ghost of a chance to seize his knife and rush Cunningham as well as whoever might be outside.

To take his eyes from the man was to risk his life. To refuse to answer the knock was to take another risk. The knock came again, sharp and peremptory. A hand tried the door. And there was a tiny sound by the window, as if other Strangers were without, peering in suspiciously and ready to fling their flying knives at a hint of danger.

8

Maria defied Cunningham without words. And Cunningham saw her father's hand stealing to a part of her dress where a weapon might be concealed. Sweat came out on his forehead. He could not shoot, and in another instant——

Then the defiance in her eyes turned to pleading and the deliberate wordless reiteration of the thing he had read in her face before. Cunningham spoke suddenly in a fierce whisper.

"I love you!" he cried softly and desperately. "Do you think I will let harm come to your father?"

The terror faded from her eyes and without a sound she clasped her father's hands fast in her own, though still before him. Stephan stood tense, watching Cunningham through eyes that showed nothing whatever.

Cunningham turned his head.

"Who's there?" he called. The answer was an anticlimax.

"Gray," said Gray's voice dryly. "I say—if you want to send any mail or telegrams, you'd better give them to me. I think they'd be opened, here."

"I know they would," Cunningham growled. "But I won't have anything to go out. Anything else? I'm in bed," he added as an afterthought.

"No. Nothing else." Gray's tone was very dry. Cunningham heard his footsteps retreating.

He silently picked up Stephan's knife and handed it back. He replaced his pistol in his pocket.

"It's dangerous to talk here," he said grimly. "I suppose these partitions are thin. Let me come up to the hills tomorrow. I'll tell you anything I can to help you. But please don't kill anybody else until I've had time to explain. Don't you understand that you can't get away with that sort of thing in the United States? Where did you come from, anyhow?"

Stephan smiled faintly. He ignored the whisper to Maria of a moment before. He suddenly reached over and put his hand on Cunningham's shoulder.

"Good man," he said gravely. "We will talk to you, yes. But we will not tell you anything. Come up into the hills tomorrow. We will kill nobody else until you say."

"But—I tell you you mustn't kill anybody at any time," protested Cunningham anxiously. "You can't get away with it. Don't you understand?"

"No," said Stephan. He spread out his hands in a confession of despair. "We do not understand anything! Maria says you are our friend. We need a friend. Else we die. And if you do not help us———"

Cunningham stared from one to the other, but it was hard to think of anything when he looked at Maria. He had taken the Strangers seriously enough when he knew of the first man's being killed. Now it looked as if he was called upon to prevent deadly serious trouble in the hills.

"I'll try," he said hopelessly. "Yes, I'll try. Maria———"

The color mounted in her cheeks. Then she seemed to summon all her pride and met his eyes fairly. They told him many things, her eyes.

"I—I will wait for you," she told him. And in the words she said much more than the words themselves.

Cunningham was tingling all over, at the same time that he felt a curious sense of absurdity in escorting callers to the window instead of to the door. But before they reached it a head appeared there. It was that of the young Stranger who had been the first to appear from the woods that afternoon.

"The sheriff," he whispered. "He came. We hit him on the head. Shall we kill him?"

"No!" said Cunningham sharply. "Tie him up until you get clear away. Did he see you coming up to my window?"

"No." The young man shrugged and disappeared. There were whispered instructions below. To Cunningham it seemed that the whispers were in a strange tongue. Maria and her father slipped out. Then there were little rustlings below. The ladder, probably, being taken down and carried elsewhere, and the marks it had made in the earth erased.

Cunningham sank into a chair and stared before him. His blood was still pounding in his veins. And Maria had glanced back at him as she disappeared from view. But there was no denying that a tremendous and unwelcome responsibility had been thrust upon him.

They were foreigners. They must be. They did not understand the laws of the United States—and they were hated now and would soon be subject to persecution. Why, otherwise, did Vladimir bribe the sheriff and try to keep both Gray and Cunningham away from the Strange People? Why, otherwise, had such unreasoning hatred been expressed that morning in Bendale?

And it was up to Cunningham to prevent a wholesale tragedy. For some unknown reason they believed that he was their friend. They would not kill anyone until he had spoken to them. That was the promise Stephan had made in their behalf,—and yet they were not bloodthirsty. He had said they only wished to be let alone, and he could not understand that that was the surest way to be thoroughly investigated. They depended now upon Cunningham. Before, without a counselor, they had killed. Now, unless Cunningham aided them, they would kill again. And Cunningham felt that the responsibility of human lives was more than he had bargained for.

Adventure was all very well, and romance was all very well, but this was different and in deadly earnest. And Cunningham could not feel any sense of superiority to them, as most men feel toward most uninformed foreigners. They were unlike him, but they were certainly not inferior to him. They knew less, but they gave no indication of lesser intelligence. And Maria——

Cunningham stood up, a trifle pale.

"Well," he muttered, "I asked for adventure and I guess I've got it."

There was another knock on the door.

"What is it?" he demanded. He wanted to be alone to think.

""Gray," said a dry voice. "Have you gotten out of bed, Cunningham?"

Cunningham opened the door.

"I came in," said Gray dryly, "to mention that Vladimir went through my room while I was gone. One key will unlock any door in this sort of hotel."

"He went through mine, too," said Cunningham abstractedly.

"And also," said Gray still more dryly, "to mention that the partitions here are very thin and that I heard all of the conversation just now."

Cunningham looked up with a start.

"I knocked on your door," Gray added, smiling cryptically, "because I knew you wouldn't open it. I was doing what I could to cement their confidence in you. Are you going to help them?"

"I guess I've got to try," said Cunningham grimly. "But I wish I knew what to do."

"Keep them from killing," Gray told him with sudden sharpness. "And also, keep them out of jail. You've got to do it, Cunningham! There'll be hell to pay in those hills if you don't. These people are scared. That's why they killed that man we saw on the train. And they will be worse scared of

Vladimir. He hasn't gone, and if I can read faces he's planning devilment for them. I tell you there'll be wholesale killings in the hills unless you go up there! Stay with them. Argue with them. Educate them if you must. But keep them from killing anybody!"

"And who," asked Cunningham grimly, "is going to keep Vladimir from starting something?"

Gray spread out his hands. Then he said curtly, "Look here. I tell you nothing———"

"Just like most other people," interpolated Cunningham none too cordially.

"———nothing," went on Gray, ignoring the interruption, "but I can promise that you won't get into trouble through trying to keep the peace."

"You're a detective?"

"No," snapped Gray. "I'm not. But I can promise that much."

"All those who have made mysteries of themselves so far," observed Cunningham grimly, "have offered me money. What do you offer?"

Gray stopped short. He seemed to realize for the first time just what sort of a predicament Cunningham was in, hopelessly at sea regarding the motives of every person in the extraordinary triangle.

"Advice," he said soberly after an instant. "I'll offer you advice. That girl is devilish pretty and I heard what you said to her. And it's insanity to say it, but—either avoid her entirely or marry her at once. And I mean at once! I've a reason for warning you."

And just as he put his hand on the knob of the door there was a scream on the ground outside. Maria had screamed. There was a crashing of glass, and as Cunningham hurled himself to his feet a shot followed, which was sickeningly loud and reverberated horribly in the stillness.

Then Vladimir's voice came purringly from a spot near by, as if he were gloating to himself, "Ha! I got her!"

9

Start of Part 2 (April, 1928 *Weird Tales* magazine)

"Rebellion was in every line of her figure."

9

With a face like death Cunningham flung through the door. He sped down the steps with his heart, it seemed, stopped dead. There were sounds behind him and angry voices. Gray roaring at Vladimir, perhaps. But Cunningham could think of nothing but Maria.

The darkness smote his eyes like a blow. He stumbled and fell, then started up, crying out wildly.

A figure flitted up to him and put a soft hand over his mouth.

"Hush! Hush! I am safe," she whispered breathlessly. "He saw us about the sheriff, and fired. When he saw the sheriff fall he thought I was killed. Hush!"

Cunningham's arms were about her and he kissed her in an ecstasy of relief.

"If he'd killed you!" he gasped. "If he'd killed you!"

Feet thundered indoors.

"I must go!" she whispered swiftly. "Please!"

She thrust him away and fled. Figures were waiting for her. She joined them, and all melted into nothingness beneath the trees. Then Gray stumbled outside with his hand in Vladimir's collar.

"Did he get her, Cunningham?" he cried shakenly. "If he did, I swear I'll fling him to them! Did he get her?"

"N-no," said Cunningham unevenly. He wiped the sweat off his forehead. "They're all gone. But———"

He knelt beside a dark bundle on the ground. A groan came to his ears, curiously muffled. He struck a match and found the sheriff securely trussed up and blinking at the match-flame with panic-stricken eyes.

"It's the sheriff," said Cunningham. "Maybe he's hurt."

But a babble of words that began before the gag was completely out of his mouth proved that the sheriff was only scared.

"Scared green, that's all," said Gray curtly. He shook Vladimir as a terrier might shake a rat. "You thought there were burglars?" he roared. "Try to get away with that again! You aimed for that girl!"

He tossed Vladimir to the ground, wrathfully.

"What girl?" purred Vladimir, as he scrambled to his feet. "Was there a girl? Are you in communication with my brother's murderers? And helping them to escape, too? I think you will go to jail, my friend."

But Gray went indoors with Cunningham, laughing.

When day came again Cunningham awoke with the conviction that something very pleasant had happened. He puzzled vaguely over it for a long time. And then he realized that it was a thing that had come to him just before he slept and had made his heart pump faster and more loudly. When he kissed Maria, she had not struggled nor been angry. On the contrary she had lifted her lips to his. And yet it had been no practised gesture, but the response of sheer instinct to one man only.

Cunningham's heart pounded a little and he got up with a serene contentment filling him. The route to romance had led him to happiness, he was sure.

He went downstairs and went out on the porch just to look up at the hills in which he would find her presently.

Vladimir was there, talking to a newcomer whose clothing and air confirmed the guess that he was a servant. But not an ordinary servant. His face was gross and stupid where Vladimir's was keen and cruel, but his features had no less of instinctive arrogance, though veiled by servility at the moment.

Vladimir's lips twitched into a snarl of hatred when he saw Cunningham, and he spoke to his servant. The man looked at Cunningham and scowled.

But Cunningham went indoors and had breakfast joyously. Then he started out to find Maria. Technically, as he reflected, he was compounding a felony in going to the Strange People to advise them how to keep out of the clutches of the law. Some of them had been involved in the killing of Vladimir's brother. But Cunningham beamed as he clambered up the steep hillside toward those mysterious thickets in which the Strange People lurked.

He had gone up perhaps half the way when he heard a faint rustling behind him. He turned and shouted, thinking it a Stranger who would lead him to Stephan and Maria. But the rustling stopped. After a little while he went on, frowning. Later the rustling began again, somewhat nearer.

And then Cunningham heard whistles far off in the thickets. He heard other rustlings, as if men were moving swiftly through the undergrowth. These last sounds came from both sides of him. And then he came suddenly upon a young Stranger, running headlong toward him with his hand on his knife-hilt. The Stranger lifted his hand, unsmilingly, and ran on.

"Stephan," cried Cunningham; "where is he?"

The runner waved for Cunningham to continue as he was going and disappeared. The mysterious sounds continued, to right and to left. Then everything was abruptly very still.

Cunningham halted uncertainly. There was no trace of a path anywhere. The earth fell away sharply at one side but he had lost all sense of direction and did not know which way to go. Then he heard a thrashing below him as if someone were moving rapidly to cut him off.

Then there was the sound of panting near by and a small boy ran into view. He was a young Stranger, an aquiline-nosed, brown-eyed youngster with the legs of a race-horse.

"Hi, there," shouted Cunningham. "Where's Stephan?"

The boy gasped in relief and flew toward him. He thrust a bit of paper into Cunningham's hand and stood panting. Cunningham unrolled the scrap. On it was written in awkward letters:

> "Someone follows to kill you. What will happen if we kill him?"

Cunningham started. Vladimir! He'd sent his servant to bushwhack him.

"They'll hang," he said grimly. "Tell them not to do it."

The boy nodded and started off.

"Wait!" called Cunningham. "Will they stop, since I've said so?"

"No," panted the boy. "They kill him already, I think."

He sped away, down toward the spot where the thrashing in the bushes sounded as if someone were trying to head Cunningham off. Cunningham clenched his fists and ran after him, determined to stop the foolishness.

The boy vanished suddenly. A figure started up.

"Wait! He lives yet! Wait!"

But Cunningham plunged on, not understanding. He only hoped to be in time to keep the Strangers from worse trouble than they were already in.

He burst through a thicket as warning cries sounded suddenly from all sides. And there was Vladimir's servant, staring stupidly about him in sudden fright at the sound of many voices. He was waist-high in brushwood. He swerved in panic at the sound of Cunningham's rush; then his face lighted with ferocity. With lightning quickness he had leveled a weapon and fired.

Cunningham's life was due to the fact that he had just tripped upon one of the innumerable small boulders strewn all over the slopes. He was falling as the bullet left the gun. He felt a searing pain in his left shoulder and crashed to the ground. Maria's voice shrilled in anguish.

"Dead! He is killed!"

The breath was knocked out of Cunningham, but he struggled to shout that he was all right, and was afraid to because the servant might pot at him again.

But then he heard half a dozen little metallic clangings, like the rattle of steel knife-blades on rock. The air was full of minor whirrings. And then he heard a sudden agonized bellow, like the roaring of a wounded bull. And then a man screaming in horrible terror.

10

There was an air of formality, even of solemnity, in the gathering that faced Cunningham several hours later. A full two hundred Strangers were gathered in a little glade with slanting sides that formed a sort of amphitheater. Scouts were hidden in the woods beyond.

And Maria was there, with a white and stricken face which dashed Cunningham's joyous mood. Vladimir's servant was there too, ashen with dread and with a crude bandage about his arm where a throwing-knife had gone through his muscles as he tried to shoot Cunningham a second time. And Stephan, Maria's father, with his features worn and very weary.

Cunningham's shoulder had been dressed with crushed plantain-leaves. It was a tiny wound at best, hardly worth more than adhesive plaster. The bullet had barely nicked the skin, but Maria had wept over it as she bound it up.

Cunningham had felt that this was no time for common sense. He knew.

"I love you," he whispered as she bent down above him.

Brimming eyes met his for an instant.

"And I love you," she said with a queer soft fierceness. "I tell you, because I will never see you again. I love you!"

Cunningham felt a nameless dread. Stephan looked at him with dreary, resolute eyes. Maria's lips were pinched and bloodless. The Strangers regarded him with somber faces which were not unfriendly, but perturbingly sympathetic.

The gathering seemed to be something like a court. The women were gathered around the outer edges. The men stood about a rock on which Stephan had seated himself. Maria stood beside him. Cunningham found himself thrust gently forward.

"My friend," said Stephan wearily, "you find us gathered in council. Men say that you kissed my daughter, Maria."

Cunningham flushed, then stood straight.

"I did," he said evenly. "I ask your permission to marry her. Is it a crime for me to speak to her first and have her answer?"

Stephan shook his head wearily.

"No. No crime. And if you were one of us I would be glad. I think you are a man. I would join your hands myself. But you are not of our people."

"And who are you," demanded Cunningham, "that I am not fit to marry into?"

Stephan's voice was gentle and quaintly sympathetic.

"We have killed one man who knew the answer to that question," he said in the teasing soft unfamiliar accent that all the Strange People had. "We do not wish to kill you. And you are not unfit to marry my daughter. My daughter, or any of us, is not fit to marry you."

Cunningham shook his head.

"Let me be the judge of that."

Again Stephan made a gesture of negation.

"I think you are our friend," he said heavily. "We need a friend of those who are not like us. We may die because we have not such a friend. But you must come here no more. What says the council?"

A murmur went up about the amphitheater—a murmur of agreement. Cunningham whirled with clenched fists, expecting to see hostile faces. Instead, he saw friendly sorry ones.

"He must not come again," ran the murmur all about the crowd, in the faint and fascinating dialect that could not ever be identified. Men gazed at Cunningham with a perturbing sympathy while they banished him.

"But why?" demanded Cunningham fiercely. "I am your friend. I came hundreds of miles because the picture of Maria drew me. I refused offers of bribes. That man"—he pointed at Vladimir's servant—"tried to kill me only today, only because I am your friend. And what have I asked of you? If Maria tells me to go, I will go. But otherwise——"

Stephan put his hand on Cunningham's shoulder.

"You must not come again," he said quietly, "because Maria loves you also. Our people know such things quickly. She has said that she loves you. And we dare not let our women marry any man but one of ourselves. It is not that we hate you. We kept that man from killing you today, and we would have killed him if you said so. We will kill him for you now, if you tell us. But we dare not let one of our women marry you. So you must go."

"Will Maria tell me to go?" demanded Cunningham fiercely.

"Yes," said Maria, dry-lipped. "Go! Oh-h-h-h. Go, if you love me!"

She flung herself down upon the grass and sobbed. Some of the women murmured to each other and one or two moved forward and patted her shoulders comfortingly.

"She tells you to go," said Stephan wearily, "because we would have to kill you otherwise."

"But why? Why?" demanded Cunningham desperately.

Stephan rose from his seat and spread out his hands.

"Because no woman can ever keep a secret from the man she loves," he said wearily. "Some day she would tell you who we are. And then you would hate her and hate us. You would turn from her in horror, and you would denounce us. And we would die, swiftly. I am not happy, my son. Maria is my daughter and I would see her happy. But some day she would tell you who we are——"

Cunningham found himself being crowded gently away from Maria. He thrust himself fiercely against the pressure.

"But who are you?" he cried savagely. "Dammit, I don't care who you are! You're making her cry! Let me pass! Let me get——"

Stephan made a gesture. With the quickness of lightning Cunningham was seized by a hundred hands. He fought like a fiend against the innumerable grips that clasped his hands, his arms, his feet. But they were too many. He stopped his struggling, panting, and stared raging at Stephan.

"We give you a gift," said Stephan quietly. "Gold, my son. Much gold. Because if Vladimir tells our secrets we will all be killed, and he threatens to tell."

"I don't want your money," panted Cunningham savagely. "I want this silly mystery ended! I want Maria! I want——"

"Go in peace," said Stephan drearily.

Cunningham was laid upon the ground and tied fast. He struggled with every ounce of his strength, but in vain. The Strange People were too many and too resolute. But they seemed to take pains not to injure him. Indeed, when they put him in a litter and started off with him, there seemed to be a consistent effort by the bearers not to make him even uncomfortable.

Cunningham raged and tore at his bonds. Then he subsided into a savage silence. His lips were set into a grim firmness. Maria sobbing upon the grass ... this abominable sympathy for him....

The litter stopped. They took him out and cut his bonds. They offered him the bags of hammered gold-pieces again.

"I don't want them," he said with grim politeness. "I warn you, I'm coming back."

The leader of his escort was the young man who had first come out of the woods the first time Cunningham had seen the Strangers. He nodded gravely.

"I know," he said quietly. "I loved a girl not of our people, last year."

The litter-bearers had vanished into the woods. Cunningham matched at a straw of hope. Perhaps here was a friend, or even a source of help.

"You understand," he said in a hurried, eager undertone. "Perhaps we can———"

"I gave her up," said the young Stranger quietly. "My people would have killed her if I had married her. You see, I might have told her."

He shrugged and pointed off through the woods.

"Coulters is there," he said gravely. "You would not take gold. I am sorry. But we think you are a man."

"I'm coming back," said Cunningham grimly.

The Stranger nodded and touched the hilt of his knife regretfully. He swung away and vanished in the underbrush.

Cunningham started toward Coulters. He knew they would be watching him. But perhaps a quarter of a mile on the way he stopped. He heard nothing and saw nothing. He slipped aside into the woods. And he had gone no more than a dozen paces before there was a little golden glitter in a ray of the dying sun. A knife had flashed past his face not two feet away. He turned back, raging.

Later he tried again. And again a warning knife swept across the path before him.

11

Cunningham had nearly reached the valley in which the hotel was built when he saw Gray below him, climbing sturdily up into the eyrie of the Strange People. Gray had a rifle slung over his shoulder.

"Gray!" shouted Cunningham.

Gray stared and abruptly sat down and mopped his forehead. He waited for Cunningham to reach him.

"Damn you, Cunningham," he said expressionlessly, "I like you, you know, for all I think we may be working against each other. And word's just gone in to Bendale that you've been killed by the Strangers. I was going up in hopes of getting to you before they wiped you out. And I already had cold chills down my back, thinking of the knife that nearly went into it yesterday."

"I'm safe enough," said Cunningham bitterly, "but I'm run out of the hills."

"Best thing, maybe," said Gray. "I'm hoping, but I think there'll be fighting there tonight. A posse's going to raid the Strangers after dark."

"*I'm* going to raid the hills tonight," said Cunningham fiercely, "and bring Maria away with me. I'll marry her in spite of all the Strangers in creation."

Gray grunted as he heaved to his feet. "You're a fool, Cunningham, and I'm another. If you go, I go too. I might learn something, anyhow."

Cunningham poured out the story of what had happened to him during the day, as they made their way down to the hotel. The sole objection to him lay in the fact that if Maria loved him, some day she would tell him who the Strangers were. And she did love him. Vladimir was the only outsider who knew their secret and he was threatening to disclose it, on what penalty Cunningham did not know.

"Maybe," said Gray quietly, "it would be a good thing if Vladimir did tell what he knows. But I suspect he won't, and for your sake I'd like to see you safely married to that girl you're so keen about before he did start to talk. I'm with you tonight, Cunningham."

"Better stay behind," said Cunningham curtly. "They'll be watching for me."

"No," said Gray quietly. "I sent some wires today and they may not be strong enough. Two of us might get her out where one wouldn't. And I'm thinking that if you do marry her and she does tell you the secret of the Strangers, it might avert a tragedy. I've done all I can without certain knowledge. Now, watch your tongue when we reach the hotel."

Cunningham ignored the raging astonishment with which Vladimir saw him, and was savagely amused at the worriment the man showed. Vladimir had sent his servant after Cunningham to kill him, and had been so certain of the attainment of that object that he had already broadcast a tale of Cunningham's death which laid it at the Strangers' door.

Cunningham waited for darkness. He was sure he had been watched back to the hotel. But after darkness was complete and before the moon rose he and Gray slipped secretly out of the house. They struck off down the valley, and when the monstrous ball of the full moon floated over the hills to the east, they made their way beneath thick trees, lest the moonlight show them to hidden watchers. They had gone perhaps a mile when Gray pointed suddenly upward.

Far, far up, where a tree-grown peak ended in a bald and rocky knob, fires were burning. Plainly visible in the clear night air, it could be seen that there were many fires and many people about them. Through the stillness, too, there came half-determinate sounds which might have been singing, or chanting, or some long-continued musical wailing.

The moon was shining down upon the valley, with its tidy New England farmhouses—upon Coulters, where uncomfortable rural police officers tried to convince themselves that they would be quite safe in dealing with the Strange People—upon Bendale, with its electric lights and once-a-week motion picture theater. And the same moonlight struck upon a ring of fires high up in the mountains where the Strangers moved and crouched. Old women gave voice to the shrill lament that was floating thinly through the air.

Gray glanced once at Cunningham's face and if he had been about to speak, he refrained. Cunningham was making grimly for the hills.

The woods were dark. The two men crept through long tunnels of blackness, where little speckles of moonlight filtered through unexpectedly and painted the tree-trunks in leopard-spots. The valley had been calm, but as they climbed, the wind began to roar over their heads, rushing among the tree-branches with a growling sound. That noise masked the sound of their movements. Once they saw one of the Strangers cross a patch of clear moonlight before them. He was moving softly, listening as he half trotted, half walked.

"Sentry," whispered Gray.

Cunningham said nothing. They went on, and heard voices murmuring before them in a foreign tongue. They halted and swung to the right. Perhaps two hundred yards on they tried again to continue up toward the heights. A crashing in the underbrush made them freeze. A Stranger trotted within five paces of them, peering about him cautiously. Only their immobility saved them from detection.

When he had gone they made for the spot from which he had come. It was breathless work because at any instant a liquid little glitter in the moonlight—a throwing-knife—might be the only herald of a silent and desperate attack.

But they made their way on and upward. It seemed as if they had passed through the ring of sentries. The trees grew thinner. The wind roared more loudly above their heads. And suddenly they saw the glow of many fires before them.

If they had gone carefully before, now they moved with infinite pains to make no noise. A single voice was chanting above the wind's screaming. Gray listened and shook his head.

"I thought I knew most languages by the sound of them," he whispered, "or could guess at the family anyhow. I worked on Ellis Island once. But I never heard that one."

They went down on their hands and knees for the last hundred yards. Then they could see. And Cunningham stared with wide eyes, while Gray swore in whispers, shaking with excitement.

There were a dozen huge bonfires placed in a monster circle twenty yards across. They roared fiercely as the flames licked at the great logs they fed upon. And the wind was sweeping up from the valley and roaring through them and around them and among them.

The rushing of the wind and the roaring of the fires made a steady, throbbing note that was queerly hypnotic. The flames cast a lurid light all around, upon the trees, and the rocks, and the Strange People, and the vast empty spaces where the earth fell away precipitously.

A single aged man chanted in the center of the twelve huge beacons. He was clad in a strange, barbaric fashion such as Cunningham had never seen before. And the Strange People had clasped hands in a great circle that went all about the blazes, and as the old man chanted they trotted steadily around and around without a pause or sound.

The old man halted his chant and cried a single sentence in that unknown tongue. From the men in the circle came a booming shout, as they sped with gathering speed about the flames. Again he cried out, and again the booming, resonant shout came from the men.

"The sunwise turn," panted Gray. "*Widdershins!* It's magic, Cunningham, magic! In New Hampshire, in these days!"

But Cunningham was thinking of no such things as magic, white or black. He was searching among the running figures for Maria. But he did not see her. The barbaric garb of the Strangers confused his eyes. That costume was rich and splendid and strange and utterly beyond belief in any group of people only eight miles from a New England mill-town with an accommodation train once a day.

"Magic!" cried Gray again in a whisper. "Cunningham, nobody'll believe it! They won't, they daren't believe it! It's impossible!"

But Cunningham was lifting himself up to search fiercely for a sight of the girl he had found at the end of the route to romance and to high adventure. Here were strange sights that matched any of the imaginative novels on which aforetime he had fed his hunger for romance. Here was a scene such as he had imagined in the midst of posting ledgers and day-books in a stuffy office on Canal Street. And Cunningham did not notice it at all, because he was no longer concerned with adventure. He had found that. He was fiercely resolved now to find the girl who loved him and whose love had been forbidden by the laws of the strange folk of the hills.

He saw her. Not in the circle. She was crouched down on the grass amid a group of women. Rebellion was in every line of her figure. Cunningham loosened his revolver. It was madness, but——

A shout rang out sharply. And the running line of men broke and milled. Cunningham saw a hundred hands flash to as many knife-hilts. He saw the sheriff and four frightened-looking constables come plunging out of the brushwood, shouting something inane about halting in the name of the law. There was a shout and a scream, and then a man's voice raised itself in a wild yell of command and entreaty. Cunningham's own name was blended in a sentence in that unintelligible language.

The Strangers darted for the encircling woods. The women vanished, Maria among them. There was only a blank space in the open lighted by monster flames, and the sheriff and two constables struggling with a single figure of the Strangers.

"Go git 'em!" roared the sheriff, holding fast to the captive. "Git 'em! They're scared. Ketch as many as ye kin!"

Cunningham felt Gray holding him down in an iron grasp.

"Don't be a fool!" rasped Gray in a whisper. "It's too late! The Strangers got away, all but one."

The other men were racing about here and there. They found nothing but a bit of cloth here, and a woman's embroidered cap there, left behind in the sudden flight.

The struggle in the open space ceased abruptly. The sheriff triumphantly called to the others.

"I got one now! Dun't be scared! We got a hostage!" He reared up and yelled to the surrounding forest: "Dun't ye try any o' your knife-throwin' tricks! This feller we got, if we dun't get down safe, he dun't neither! Dun't ye try any rescuin'!"

He bent down to jerk his prisoner upright. And Cunningham heard him gasp. He chattered in sudden stillness and the others huddled about him.

"Dead!" gasped one of them.

"He stabbed hisself, I tell ye," shrilled the sheriff. "He stuck his own knife in hisself!"

The five ungainly figures stared at each other, there amidst the roaring, deserted bonfires. One of them began to whimper suddenly.

"They—they'll be throwin' their knives all the way down to the valley!" he gasped. "They'll be hidin' behind trees an' a-stabbin' at us."

The sheriff's teeth began to chatter. The others clutched their weapons and gazed affrightedly at the woods encircling them.

"We—we got to try it," gulped the sheriff, shivering. "We got to! Else they'll get guns an' kill us here. If—if ye see anything movin', shoot it! Dun't wait! If ye see anything, shoot...."

With staring, panic-stricken eyes, they made for the woods. Cunningham heard them crashing through the undergrowth in the darkness, whimpering and gasping in terror at every fancied sound.

They left behind them nothing but twelve great fires that began slowly to burn low, and a crumpled figure in barbaric finery lying with his face upturned toward the sky. It was the young Stranger who only that afternoon had told Cunningham of the girl he had loved and lost because she was not of the Strange People. He had stabbed himself when captured, rather than be taken out of the hills and forced to tell the secret of the Strangers.

12

By morning the outside valleys were up in arms. One man—the foreigner of the train—had been killed by the Strange People, and a servant of Vladimir's had disappeared among them. And witchcraft had been believed in not too long ago in those parts. The wild ceremony of the Strangers among their blazing fires was told and retold, and with one known killing to their discredit and the long-smoldering hatred they had inspired, at the end it was related as devil-worship undiluted. Something out of Scripture came to be put in it and men told each other—and firmly believed—that children were being kidnaped and sacrificed to the Moloch out of the Old Testament. The single Stranger who had been killed became another human sacrifice, confusingly intermingled with the other and more horrible tale, and there was no doubt in the mind of any of the local farmers that the Strangers planned unspeakable things to all not of their own kind.

Had any Stranger been seen without the hills, he would have been mobbed by an hysterical populace. Sober, God-fearing men huddled their families together and stood guard over them. Women watched their children with their husbands' shotguns in their hands. Wilder and ever wilder rumors sped with lightning speed from homestead to homestead in the valleys.

And all this was done without malice. The native-born people had distrusted the Strange People because they were strange. They disliked them because they were aloof. And they came to hate them because they were mysterious. It is always dangerous to be a mystery. The story of what the sheriff and his four constables had seen among the fires on the heights became enlarged to a tale of unspeakable things. It would have required no more than a leader with a loud voice to mobilize a mob of farmers who would have invaded the hills with pitchforks and shotguns to wipe out the Strange People entirely.

They did not fear the Strangers as witches, but as human beings. They feared them as possible kidnapers of children to be killed in the inhuman orgies the fire-ceremony had become in the telling. They had no evidence of such crimes committed by the Strangers. But there is no evidence of kidnaping against the gipsies, yet many people suspect them of the same crime. Had any man spoken the truth about the Strangers, he would have been suspected of horrible designs—of being in sympathy with them. And because of the totally false tales that sprang up like magic about their name, to be suspected of sympathy with the Strangers was to court death.

Cunningham's rage grew. Gray shrugged and rode furiously to Bendale to send more telegrams. Vladimir went about softly, purring to himself, and passed out bribes lavishly to those who could be bribed, and told lies to those who preferred to be suborned in that way.

He was holding back the plans of mobbing. The sheriff, acting on his orders, broke up every group of wild-talking men as soon as it formed. But Vladimir held the Strange People in the hollow of his palm. Half a dozen murmured words, and the men who had taken his lavished money would stand aside and let the simmering terror of the countryside burst out into the frenzy of a mob. And then the hills would be invaded by Christian men who would ferret out the Strangers and kill them one by one in the firm belief that they were exterminating the agents of Satan and the killers of innumerable children.

It did not matter that Vladimir's hold was based on lies. The lies were much more exciting than the truth. The truth was dull and bare. The Strangers had been dancing about the fires. The constables had rushed out and they had fled, without attempting to resist or harm their attackers. One of them had stabbed himself when caught. And the truth was mysterious enough, and inexplicable enough, but it did not compare with the highly colored tales of human sacrifice and heathen orgies that had been embroidered upon the original tale.

Cunningham was inevitably in the thick of all these rumors. Men came rushing with news. A Stranger had been seen lurking about where children were playing. He was instantly suspected of planning to kidnap one of them. He had been shot at and now was being chased by dogs. A Stranger had stopped a doctor in the road and asked for bandaging for an injured arm. He had been shot by one of the constables the night before. Other Strangers guarded him lest the doctor try to arrest him while he dressed the wound.

That was in the morning. As the day went on the reports became more horrible. It became clear that if any Stranger showed his face he would be shot at as if he were a mad dog.

Word came from one place. Two Strangers had been seen and fired on. They vanished, leaving a trail of blood. From another place came another report. An old Strange woman had come out of the hills, to beg for medicines for their wounded. Dogs were set on her as she screamed her errand. She fled, and knives came hurtling from the brushwood, killing or wounding the dogs that were in pursuit.

Gray had promised much. With a drawn and anxious face he had told Cunningham that this day help must come. His telegrams must have produced results. They must have had some effect! He had long since dropped his pretense that his only mission in the hills was the study of the Strange People's dialect. He was off in Bendale, struggling with a telephone, pleading with a long-distance operator to give him a connection to somewhere—anywhere outside.

Noon came and passed. The afternoon waned, with the inhabitants of the valley growing more and more hysterical in their hatred of the Strange People, and more and more detailed and convinced about the horrors they ascribed to them. The wholly imaginary menace of the Strangers was making it more and more difficult to prevent the formation of a mob. Men raved, wanting to protect their children by wiping out the hill folk. Women grew hysterical, demanding their annihilation.

Cunningham went to Vladimir. Vladimir blinked at him and licked his lips.

"Your servant is a prisoner among the Strange People," said Cunningham, coldly. "I'm authorized to say he'll be killed if a mob enters the hills."

Vladimir smiled, and all his cruelty showed when he smiled.

"How are you authorized to speak for them?"

"Let that go," said Cunningham grimly. "He's alive and safe, but he won't be if that mob goes in."

The sheriff came in hurriedly.

"Mr. Vladimir——" he began.

Cunningham cut into his report with some sharpness.

"Sheriff, the Strange People are holding Vladimir's servant prisoner, as a hostage. They'll kill him if you raid the hills again."

Vladimir laughed.

"He is vastly mistaken, sheriff. I had a servant here, it is true. But I sent him to Boston, on a mission. And I had word from him yesterday that he was quite safe and attending to my orders."

He blinked at Cunningham and moved close to him.

"Fool," he murmured gently, so that the sheriff could not hear, "do you think his life counts any more than yours?"

The sheriff glared at Cunningham hatefully.

"Tryin' to scare me, eh?" he rumbled. "I got enough on you to arrest you. You're in thick with them Strangers, you are. I reckon jail's the best place for you. You won't get no chance to talk about bribes there."

Cunningham felt himself growing white with fury. His threat to Vladimir had been a bluff, and Vladimir had shown complete indifference to the fate of the man he had sent to murder Cunningham. But there was one thing he would not be indifferent to.

"You try to arrest me," he said softly to the sheriff, "and I'll blow your head off. And as for you, Vladimir"—he made his tone as convincing as he could—"I just tell you that you'd better call that mob off or I'll tell them who the Strangers are and where they came from!"

Vladimir's eyes flamed close to madness, while his cheeks went ashen.

"So they told you!" he purred. "Sheriff, go to the door. I wish to speak to this man privately."

The sheriff, rumbling, moved away.

"My friend," murmured Vladimir softly, "now I shall have to kill you. Not myself, of course, because that would be illegal. And dangerous. But I give you news. Today, while you and Gray were outside, a little note was tossed into your window. I heard the breaking glass and found it. It was from a girl, who signed, 'Maria.' She said that she loved you and would wait for you at a certain spot to flee with you."

Cunningham's heart stopped. Vladimir laughed at his expression.

"Oh, she was met," murmured Vladimir. "She was met—and arrested. She is held fast. And tonight a story will go about and the women of the neighborhood will learn where she is. She is in the hotel here, safely bound. With such a tale as will be spread about, do you not think the women will pull down the whole hotel to tear her in bits? Now do you go and tell the secret of the Strangers! No one will believe you. But you believe me!"

He tossed a scrap of paper to Cunningham. And Cunningham knew that the story was true.

"Now," said Vladimir, purring, "I shall give orders that you be arrested. If you are taken, she will be torn to bits. And that is how I kill you, my friend. That is how I kill you! For I do not want anyone to live who will remember or believe the secret of the Strangers."

13

Then the news took a definitely dangerous turn. A farmer who was hastening to Coulters was stopped by a band of Strangers. They had taken his shotgun and shells from him, contemptuously tossing him half a dozen of the square lumps of gold. The gold would pay for the gun ten times over, but men raged. Another man came in foaming at the mouth, with a similar tale. He had seen a Stranger and raised his gun to fire as at a wild beast. A knife had flicked at him and gone through the fleshy part of his arm. They took his gun and shells, leaving gold to pay for them.

No one saw anything odd in firing on the Strangers at sight. But everyone grew hysterically excited at the thought of the Strangers taking guns with which to shoot back. Then a man rode up on a lathered horse, shouting hoarsely that twenty Strangers had raided a country store some six miles away. They had appeared suddenly. When they left they took half a dozen shotguns—the whole stock—three rifles, and all the ammunition in the store. They left gold to pay for the lot.

Cunningham heard all this as one would hear outside sounds during a nightmare. He was like a madman. He would have gone rushing through the place in search of Maria but that it was still broad daylight and there were twenty or more armed men in the place, all mad with excitement and fury. As it was, Cunningham was in a cold, clear-headed rage. He went to his own room and packed his pockets with cartridges.

Vladimir was right in one respect. The natives were in no mood to listen to the truth. They would believe nothing that he told them. He was suspect, in any event. They classed him with the Strangers, and they classed the Strangers with the beasts. Fighting such men was not fighting law and order. The sheriff was bribed. The rest were wild with rage and terror. They did not know they were catspaws for Vladimir. Even the sheriff probably knew but little of Vladimir's plans.

He went into Gray's room and searched for a possible second revolver. As he pawed grimly among Gray's possessions he heard the sheriff speaking, through a partition. Gray's room was next to that occupied by Vladimir, and Cunningham abruptly realized how Gray had obtained much information.

"I'm doin' my best to hold 'em," the sheriff was saying anxiously, "but it's gettin' to be a tough job. I'd better send for militia——"

"Fool!" snarled Vladimir. "What do I give you money for? There will be no fighting! We will march into the hills. We will pen up these folk—surround them. If your mob kills a few, what harm? Afterward you shall pick out your murderers—as many as you choose! They will confess to anything you choose, after I have spoken to them. And then the rest of the Strangers will move away. They will go away forever, with me! I will take them!"

"But it looks bad——"

"They will lick my boots," rasped Vladimir. "They will crawl upon their knees and beg me for mercy. And I will give you four men to hang. They will confess to their crime. And I will take the rest away."

Cunningham nodded grimly. At least this clarified the situation a little. Vladimir was afraid of the Strangers' secret becoming known. He only wanted to get them away. If he could find Maria and she would tell him, and Gray brought the help he had promised——

Cunningham was not thinking for himself, except as his liberty meant safety for Maria, and secondarily for the Strange People. But he would have to go into every room in the hotel filled with armed and suspicious men. It was lucky he had two guns. There would surely be shooting. There would probably be a bullet or two for him.

"Now send your deputies to arrest Cunningham," snapped Vladimir on the other side of the wall. "Tell them to shoot him if he resists. He was teaching the Strangers to shoot and advising them to resist arrest. That is enough."

"I'll send a bunch," whined the sheriff uneasily. "He's a desp'rit character. Talkin' about accusin' me of takin' bribes...."

"You'll be rich for life when this is over," Vladimir purred. "Remember that!"

The door closed behind the sheriff. Cunningham grinned savagely. He was to have no chance at all. They had been sent to arrest him, after Vladimir had given him news that would ensure his resisting. He would resist, right enough! And then a wild and utterly reckless scheme sprang full-bodied into Cunningham's head.

He swung the door to—and heard a squeaking on the other side of the partition as if a closet door had been opened. And then Vladimir spoke purringly in that unknown language of the Strangers!

There could be but one person to whom he would be speaking at such a time and in that language. Cunningham's heart leaped violently. He heard voices downstairs—men coming up to arrest him in his own room.

He darted out in the hall and plunged into Vladimir's room, a ready revolver upraised. Vladimir whirled and stared into its muzzle with ashen cheeks. For once there was no purred jibe upon his lips, because Cunningham's face was the face of a killer after he had seen Maria in the clothes-closet, bound hand and foot and with a gag in her mouth. She had been staring at Vladimir in horror, but her eyes flamed at sight of Cunningham.

For the fraction of a second they gazed at each other. Then her eyes signaled frantic warning. Cunningham whirled and dashed his revolver blindly in Vladimir's face as his hand came up with an automatic. Vladimir stumbled and crashed backward to the floor.

Footsteps crashed on the steps outside. Nearly all the men in the hotel, it seemed, were coming up in a body to see to the arrest of Cunningham. But he paid no attention. He was ripping away at the gag and tearing loose the bonds that held Maria fast.

"Vladimir told me you'd been captured," he panted, "and said you'd be mobbed tonight. Now he's sent a gang to arrest me, knowing I'd resist and get myself killed. We've got to make a break for it. All right?"

Maria's eyes were like stars. Cunningham kissed her suddenly.

"My God!" he laughed shakily. "One can think of love-making even at a time like this! Listen!"

The crowd on the stairs had reached the top. They crowded down the hall before Cunningham's own door. There they hesitated, shuffling uneasily. At last a voice called loudly, "Open in the name of the law!"

There was no answer from Cunningham's empty room. They waited breathlessly. A man pounded cautiously on the panel of the door.

"Open in th' name of th' law!"

Still silence.

"M-maybe he j-jumped outer th' window," suggested someone uneasily.

"R-rush him," urged a man safely in the rear.

Cunningham and Maria, two rooms away, heard a hand laid on the other room's door. They heard it fling open with a crash and the scuttling of feet as the mob of hastily deputized men jumped to one side to be out of the way of possible bullets. Dead silence greeted them. And suddenly they crowded into the deserted place.

"Now!" said Cunningham sharply.

He darted out, Maria running with him. She fled to the stairs and down them, Cunningham two steps in the rear. A single straggler of the men who were to have arrested him remained in the hall. He turned his head stupidly at sound of their rush. His mouth dropped open, but before his shout they were half-way to the ground floor.

Cunningham stopped at the foot of the stairs to fire three times up at the ceiling of the second floor. A cloud of smoke filled the hall, and heads that had craned over the balustrade withdrew, in a panic. A dozen paces more and the fugitives were out in the roadway. Half a dozen horses were tethered there and Cunningham tore loose the reins and leaped on one. Maria sprang up lightly behind him and he kicked the animal madly with his heels. It sprang into a panic-stricken gallop and was off down the road.

They were nearly out of sight before the first of their pursuers had run out into the road behind them. Then half a dozen puffs of smoke showed that they were fired on, but an instant later they were out of sight around a bend in the road.

14

Cunningham laughed a little as the horse's hoofs clattered beneath and the white road shot past. Maria was clinging to his shoulders.

"Safe so far," he told her, "but now we have to take to the woods. The hand of every man is against us, Maria. Do you trust me to get you away?"

"Anywhere," she said softly. "You know I do."

A motorcar came racing toward them over the rough road. It was not fit going for an automobile and the car swayed and lurched from side to side with dangerous abandon. Cunningham swerved his horse out of the road. The car slowed and stopped with a screaming of brakes. Cunningham's hand fell to his weapon.

Gray tumbled out of the cloud of dust that enveloped the machine.

"Cunningham," he panted. "Just found—Vladimir had bribed the telegraph operator. None of my wires got through. Found an amateur radio fan and he sent my message. Relay League. Help's coming. By airplane. Bendale is a town of lunatics. Wild yarns have gone into it and a mob is coming out to wipe out the Strangers. They think they've been burning children. You've got to get up to the Strangers. Tell 'em about planes. Tell them to get going and keep moving or there'll be a massacre. Help's coming as fast as it can get here. But for God's sake keep them away from the mob. They'll be wiped out!"

"I'm going to get Maria away," said Cunningham defiantly. "I'm going to get her out of this state and marry her. The Strangers and anybody else can go to the devil!"

Gray, choking upon the dust he had swallowed, gasped out a raging order.

"Don't be a fool!" he cried. "Look at her clothes! She's in the Strangers' costume! You'll be spotted if you're seen, and three townships are raving crazy! A dog couldn't get away from here like that! You'll be shot at by every damned fool in three counties and arrested anywhere else you go! Get up in the hills and keep the Strangers moving! The planes may not get here until dark, and they can't land in the hills in the darkness. I'm going to meet them at Hatton Junction and guide them here. You get up in the hills and keep the Strangers moving or there'll be a massacre! That mob will even wipe out the children! Everybody's crazy! You've got to save them, Cunningham! You've got to!"

And Cunningham knew that he was telling the truth. The Strange People might not fight, if he begged them not to. To desert them would mean a tragedy in the hills. The people about them were no more accountable than so many lunatics. But to ride among the Strange People with Maria upon his saddle! ... They would know that she loved him, and they would believe that she had told him their secret. They would never let him leave the hills again alive.

It was death either way, and probably for them both. He looked at Maria and found her eyes misty with tears.

"Let me go," she said suddenly, with a sob in her throat. "You go away. I will go up to my people and tell them what this man has said. Without me, you can escape. My people will tell me to die, but you will not know who we are and you will never hate me or despise me...."

Cunningham caught her hand and laughed shortly.

"No, my dear," he said grimly. "We won't be separated. It's a choice between being shot like mad dogs or facing your people. We'll ride up into the hills. We'll tell your people that help is coming to hold off the mob. Their lives will be safe and their secret too, for all of me. And if we die, it will be decently. I've two guns for the pair of us."

He found himself laughing as he waved his hand at Gray and drove his horse at the steep slopes that led upward to the tree-clad heights in which the Strangers lurked.

As the trees closed over their heads he smiled again and swung Maria before him. He gave the horse its head and the animal dropped to a plodding walk. And they talked softly. They had but a little while to be alone and they had never talked the tender foolishness that lovers know. Now they were riding at a snail's pace upward to the stern vengeance of the Strangers upon a woman of their number who had loved outside the clan.

They spoke in whispers, not to avoid detection but because there are some things that are too tender to be spoken aloud. And their eyes spoke other things for which nobody has ever found words. Maria's arm was about Cunningham's neck and her lips were never far from his own and it seemed as if all trouble and care were very far away, though they were riding up to death.

The trees rustled above them. Birds sang all about them. And they rode through an age-old forest upon a weary horse, a scarecrow of a man with a bandaged shoulder and a girl in barbaric finery, gazing at him with tear-misted eyes. And as they rode they talked softly, and now and then they smiled, and in every speech and glance and gesture there was an aching happiness and a wistful regret.

All this was very foolish, but it was the proper and authentic conclusion for a man who has followed the route to romance and adventure to its appointed ending.

But there came a little rustling in the undergrowth beside them as they went on climbing up to the heights. Then other rustlings. Far away there was a whistle as if someone signaled. And very suddenly an arm reached out from the thick brushwood and seized the horse's bridle. One of the Strangers stepped into view and gazed steadily up into the muzzle of Cunningham's revolver.

From all about them men materialized as if by magic. No man laid a hand on any weapon. They looked at the pair upon the horse gravely, without rancor but with infinite resolution.

And Stephan, Maria's father, came into view and regarded them with weary, hopeless eyes.

"Why did you come back?" he asked in a queer and resolute despair. "You knew what we would have to do. Why did you come back?"

15

Start of Part 3 (May, 1928 *Weird Tales* magazine)

"He was hidden from view in a mass of stabbing figures."

15

The sun sank thunderously behind the mountain-range and tinted the tips of all the peaks with gold. Little fleecy clouds floated overhead in contented indolence. The wind of the heights was still. The pine-clad hills seemed very soft and restful as the shadows deepened on the eastern slopes, and contrasted strangely with the still-bright golden fields of the valleys yet unshadowed by the mountains.

Stephan held out a weary hand, pointing. A sullen column of smoke rose from a point far distant. He pointed again, where a thin wisp of vapor grew steadily thicker and denser.

"Our houses," he said bitterly. "They are being burned. Vladimir has spoken, and we die."

Cunningham clenched his fists as the sullen gray clouds rose slowly upward in the still air. Once he saw figures moving about the base of the smoke. Once he thought he heard yelling.

"I don't think he's told your secret," he said after an instant. "That's the mob. Gray promised that help would come. He said it was coming by airplane. And Vladimir——"

He told Stephan swiftly what Vladimir had said to the sheriff: that the Strangers were to be surrounded by the mob, and that then he would speak to them; that they would submit, and that some would go away in chains to be hung for the murder of his brother, and that he would take the others away with him forever; that they would follow when he spoke to them and obey him in all things.

Stephan's eyes flashed fire for a second.

"Is life so sweet or peace so dear," he quoted bitterly, "as to be purchased at the price of chains and slavery?" He stopped short. "No," he said quietly. "We will not obey him. No!"

Cunningham felt again that curious impotent bafflement. Stephan had just quoted Patrick Henry's speech to the House of Burgesses, the famous "Give me liberty or give me death" speech. And Stephan had never seen a revolver until Cunningham showed him one, nor a shotgun save at a distance and in the hands of the farmers about him. None of the Strange People were better informed. Keeping passionately to themselves, it was possible that they would never have seen a pistol if they were ignorant of them before they came mysteriously to these hills. Revolvers are not common in country places, nor are those possessed displayed.

"You see," said Stephan with a faint smile, "how I was able to spare you for a time. It is likely that we will all soon be dead. And then it does not matter if you know our secret or not."

"Tell me now," begged Cunningham. "It will make no difference to you, and it may mean everything——"

Stephan smiled slowly at Maria, who was clinging to Cunningham's arm as if she feared that at any instant he might be torn away.

"You say you do not know," he said with a wretched attempt at lightness. "Maria loves you. You would despise her if you knew. Let her be happy as long as may be." He paused and surveyed the hillside with keen eyes, then added: "We trust you. We might have killed many of that mob already. They were careless. But we have fled before them. We will keep from killing them as long as we can, because you have asked it."

"Gray will be here!" said Cunningham passionately. "He has promised! Help will come!"

Stephan shrugged his shoulders and gave a low-voiced order in the unknown tongue which the Strangers spoke among themselves.

"Help," he said in a moment more, and smiled very wearily indeed. "The soldiers will come, no doubt. And then we die indeed. We move now, my son."

Half a dozen Strangers hovered near Cunningham. They were guards, to prevent his escape at any cost. That they would kill him to keep him from getting away there was no doubt. That they hated him was totally improbable. The faces of all the Strangers wore a settled, fatalistic look. Every one was now clad in the barbaric costume they had worn about the fires the night before, as if they had abandoned all hope of pretending longer that they were of the same sort as the inhabitants of the valleys.

Cunningham followed as the Strangers moved on. Little bands of them were constantly appearing unexpectedly from the woods and joining the main body. There were quite two hundred in all when they passed over a hill-crest and settled themselves in the valley beyond.

The mob had appeared from Bendale. On horse-back, in motor-cars and in wagons drawn by teams, what seemed to be the whole population had come raging out to Coulters. The farmers of the valley had put their women-folk together and come armed with weapons, from shotguns to pitchforks. And they had surged into the hills in quest of the Strange People. All had forgotten that the only thing genuinely proved against the Strangers was the death of Valdimir's brother. All were hysterically convinced that the Strangers made a practise of kidnaping children and sacrificing adults in devilish orgies by their fires.

The belief was not unparalleled. To be peculiar is to invite suspicion. The Strangers were peculiar. Suspicion is always based on fear. What fear is more terrible than that of harm to one's children? Every unknown man or race of men has been accused of the one crime. Gipsies are not yet freed of the suspicion of kidnaping. A lurking tramp or wanderer is instantly and invariably suspected of intent to commit the same offense.

Was it odd, then, that the secretive folk of the hills had been classed as doubtful? The mysterious ceremony of the fires, as described by the ignorant and frightened constables, was capable of any interpretation. What had been doubts and vague surmises became certainties when coupled with the ceremony which was meaningless unless sinister.

Now the Strangers had withdrawn from the first of the mountain-slopes. They abandoned their homes to the mob without a struggle. The houses went up in flames. The Strangers had seen the columns of smoke rising to the sky.

Men and women wore a look of settled calm. A mob that vastly outnumbered them, and was vastly better armed, was seeking them in raging madness. They waited to die. Some of the younger men chafed at the delay in fighting. With their throwing-knives they might have picked off many of their persecutors, but Stephan had forbidden it.

They waited. Darkness fell. Through the stillness of early night came the sound of a shot, then another and another. Wild yells broke loose below.

After a long time a runner came panting to the bivouac. He had bound the embroidered sash that was part of his costume about his arm, but it was stained—a dark purple in the moonlight.

Stephan ordered another move. Uncomplainingly the Strangers rose and plodded farther into the hills. The children were weary. Fretful little cries rose from the long line. Women hushed them gently. There was little talk. Just a long line of barbarously clad people plodding with bowed heads onward, onward, onward, while a shouting, raving mob raged through the woods in quest of them.

Cunningham went with them. He had no choice, but it is doubtful if he would have done otherwise had he been able to.

Again the weary people settled for a little rest. Yells sounded faintly, far to the right. A red glow began and grew larger and became a house burning with a crackling noise in the wilderness. Cunningham saw an old man rise on one elbow and peer at the flames. His face was apathetic. Then he lay down again.

"That was my house," he said quietly to the man nearest him, and was silent.

Again came runners, panting. One man was sobbing in rage and humiliation, begging leave to plunge into the mob and die fighting—alone, if need be.

Stephan refused him gently.

"I think we die," he said grimly, "but he"—Stephan pointed at Cunningham—"has promised that help will come. I do not believe it, but we can miss no chance. We have women with us, and children. We must hold ourselves for them. While the least chance remains, we must live."

Once more came the order to move. And once more the weary march began. It had no object and it had no hope. But beneath the full moon the Strangers plodded on and on, until the baying of dogs set up behind them.

"They've sent down in the valley and got dogs!" raged Cunningham in a blend of fury and sick horror.

Stephan stroked his chin and gazed at Cunningham.

"What now, my son?" he asked.

Cunningham shook his head in despair.

"This is the end," said Stephan quietly. "I think—I think we may let you go on alone, if you wish. You may escape."

"Maria?" demanded Cunningham, very white. He would feel like a coward and a scoundrel if he deserted these people, but if he could save Maria he would do it.

"No," said Stephan. "She is my daughter and I would save her life. But if our secret is known it is best that she die quickly with the rest."

Cunningham groaned and clenched his fists.

"I stay," he said harshly. "And—I fight with you!"

Sunrise broke upon the Strangers huddled high up on a bare and windswept peak. Its first cold rays aroused them. Gradually it warmed them. And it showed them clearly to a ring of still-raging men who were made savage by the ruin they had wrought during the night. From fifty places in the hills thin columns of smoke still rose wanly to the sky, from as many heaps of ashes that had been the Strangers' homes.

And shots began to be fired from the besiegers of the Strange People. Then Vladimir rode forward on a white horse and shouted to them in that unknown language.

16

Cunningham could not understand the speech of Vladimir, nor the replies that Stephan made. Only, once Maria clung to his arm in an access of hope.

"He has not spoken!" she whispered. "He is threatening now to tell them who we are——"

Then Vladimir was shouting promises, to judge by his tone. A moment later his voice was stern.

Maria sobbed suddenly. A growl went up from the Strangers, running all about among the huddled figures.

Far away over the hills a low-toned buzzing set up. It strengthened and grew louder. A black dot hung between earth and sky. It grew larger. A second black dot appeared; a third. Wings could be seen upon the first of the airplanes. More and more appeared until there were six in all, flying in formation and winging their way steadily toward the hills.

They darted back and forth, searching. Cunningham shouted joyously.

"There they are!" he yelled. "Tell Vladimir to go to hell, Stephan! We've got help with us now!"

Vladimir had heard the sound of the engines and stared upward. Then foam appeared upon his lips and he shrieked with rage.

"There will be soldiers upon those things?" asked Stephan quietly. The Strangers were gazing up at the swooping aircraft that quartered the hills like monster hawks, in quest of the Strangers and their enemies.

"Surely," Cunningham told him joyously. "They'll carry five men apiece, with the pilots."

Stephan rose and stepped forward, where he shouted in a stentorian voice to Vladimir. Maria gasped in terror and clung close to Cunningham.

"He is—he is going to do as Vladimir says!" she cried. "Do not let him do it! Oh, do not——"

Stephan turned and spoke in a low tone in the unknown tongue of the Strangers. And where there had been rebellion among the defiant folk on the peak before he spoke, afterward there were grim smiles. Men's hands loosened the knives in their belts.

Stephan shouted again in apparent panic, pointing up to the flying things that circled suddenly above them. And Vladimir's face contorted in a grin of direst cruelty. He called over his shoulder and rode forward until he was just out of throwing-knife range. Then he shouted once more.

At Stephan's low-toned order a cloud of knives went licking through the air and fell at his horse's feet. And Vladimir grinned savagely and rode up, quite up, among the Strange People.

They cowered as he drew close to them. They crawled upon the ground as he stared savagely about him. They shook in seeming terror as he snarled a phrase or two at them. Cunningham gripped his revolver, his eyes blazing amid all his bewilderment. He had never seen such beastly cruelty upon the face of any living man. Maria clung close to him, shaking in unearthly terror.

Vladimir rode his horse toward a cowering group. They rolled away, gasping in apparent horror, as the horse was upon them. Not one lifted a finger to defend himself. They seemed stricken with utter, craven terror. They crawled abjectly upon the ground before him.

Vladimir came upon the bullet-headed servant he had sent to kill Cunningham. The man fawned up at his master, bound hand and foot as he was. Vladimir gazed at him sardonically and spoke in a purring tone. Then he deliberately shot the man dead.

The Strange People cringed. Then Vladimir saw Cunningham. He rode over and stared down with cold, beastly eyes.

"Ah, my friend," he purred. "You know the secret of my folk, you say. Perhaps you lie, but it does not matter. You saw the end of my servant, did you not? That was for failing to kill you as I ordered. Do you remember that after that you struck me?"

Cunningham's fingers itched on trigger.

"I do," he said curtly. "You'd better run away, Vladimir. My friend Gray has some unbribed officers in those planes that are going to land in a minute or so."

Vladimir laughed.

"What difference?" he asked amusedly. "My people are cowed, now. They will swear to anything I choose to tell them. All that I need to do is hand over some of them to be hanged. One or two will go for killing my servant. They will confess to whatever I say. And I will take the others away with me."

"You're sure?" asked Cunningham grimly. "Quite sure?"

"But certainly," Vladimir laughed again. "They are afraid I will tell who they are. But you—— Time is short." He glanced at Stephan and his voice rasped. "Take away his weapons!"

Stephan approached Cunningham, cowering from the menace of Vladimir's eyes. He seemed to be in the ultimate of terror, but as he drew near to Cunningham, and Vladimir could not see his face, he smiled grimly. There was no terror on his face then. He made a reassuring gesture.

"Take it!" rasped Vladimir harshly. "Disarm him!"

Stephan's lips moved but Cunningham could not quite understand what he wished to convey. But he had two revolvers and he thrust one into Stephan's hand and drew and jerked the other behind him while Stephan's body covered the movement.

"Ah," purred Vladimir as Stephan drew back and handed over the weapon. "You see it is necessary to kill you, Cunningham. My folk will take the blame for it. I shall probably let Stephan hang for your murder. They need a lesson, you understand. But I will be merciful. A bullet through the heart——"

He raised Cunningham's own revolver, but he never fired it. As his arm lifted, Cunningham's own weapon came around. But Cunningham did not fire either. There was a panted ejaculation and a dozen Strangers seemed to spring from the earth. With the savagery and directness of so many panthers they leaped upon Vladimir. He was hidden from view in a mass of savagely stabbing figures who clung to him in a grim silence. Vladimir screamed just once, and his revolver went off with a deafening explosion. One of the Strangers rolled to the ground, coughing, while he grinned in spite of his agony.

And then Vladimir fell with a crash to the ground and lay still.

There was a shout from the Strangers. Men yelled and the younger ones darted out to where their knives had been tossed before Vladimir. They came racing back with armfuls of the shining blades. They distributed them swiftly, grinning as they did so.

And in less than two minutes from the time Vladimir had ridden up to the peak where the Strangers lay barricaded, he had died and the Strangers were again lying in wait for the attack that they were sure would result in their annihilation.

But the great airplanes came coasting down heavily. Their motors shut off one by one and they zoomed to lose speed and pancaked with sudden awkwardness to the earth. This was no ideal landing-place. Three of them alighted safely. One was tilted sidewise by a sudden gust of wing and crumpled up a wing against a tree. Two others crashed their landing-gear on boulders on the rocky hillside.

Then Gray leaped out of the first to land, shouting frantically to the besiegers to fire no more. Men jumped from the others and spread themselves about the peak. They were alert grim figures with rifles which they handled with familiar ease. And Gray came running up to the embattled Strangers, his hands high above his head, and shouting that he was a friend.

17

"Planes had to land at the Junction last night," said Gray curtly to Cunningham. "Didn't get here until sunset and couldn't land in unfamiliar territory after dark, particularly this kind of territory. I went on and met them last night. We took off at sunrise. What happened? Any fighting?"

"Several of us shot," said Cunningham grimly. "Nobody killed that I know of. But every house in the hills has been looted and burnt."

"Fools!" snapped Gray. "But they'd do that.—What's that?"

He was staring at a sprawled heap on the ground.

"That was Vladimir," said Cunningham calmly. "He'd just shot his servant for failing to kill me, and was shooting me down in cold blood when the Strangers jumped him. You don't get a murder case out of this, Gray. They killed him to save my life."

"Glad of it," said Gray restlessly. "Now———"

"By the badge you've stuck on your coat," said Cunningham grimly, "you're a detective of some sort. And I suppose those chaps who came in the planes are Federal men. What do you want with the Strangers, Gray?"

Gray stirred uneasily. Then he faced Cunningham squarely.

"I'm in the immigration service," he said flatly. "These people are aliens, smuggled in. You can guess the rest of it yourself."

"I can't," said Cunningham savagely. "There's more to it than that, and they won't tell me; not even Maria."

Stephan spoke quietly. "Do you know who and what we are?"

"I do," said Gray curtly. "You're———"

Stephan stopped him with an upraised palm. His face was the color of ashes.

"Then you know," he said tonelessly, "why we prefer to die here. And since our young friend will not leave us of his own will, my young men will carry him, bound———"

"Try it," said Cunningham briefly. "If there's fighting, I fight. If Maria dies, I die. That's all."

He brought his remaining weapon into view and held it grimly.

Gray stared from one to the other.

He shrugged his shoulders almost up to his ears and waved his hands helplessly. And then he said quickly, "Since I know, and the soldiers know, there's no harm in telling Cunningham."

Maria, her lips bloodless, whispered, "Tell him. It is best."

But it was to Gray that Stephan turned. His back was toward Cunningham as he made a gesture for Gray's benefit alone. Cunningham could not see, but it seemed as if Stephan had thrust up the wide sleeve of his embroidered jacket. And Gray licked his lips and said, "Oh, my God!"

"I tell you my own story," said Stephan quietly. "The others are much the same. Twenty years ago I was the son of a village headman in Daghestan, which is in southern Russia. And there came upon me suddenly this—this thing which has made me one of the Strangers."

Gray, shuddering, nodded. Cunningham raised his head.

"What thing?" he demanded.

"My own people would have stoned me when they knew," said Stephan grimly. "My own father would have killed me. And I was a fool then. I desired still to live. I had heard whispers of this America, in which the son of the Governor of Daghestan had found a mine of gold so rich that he must work it secretly. It lay in a hidden valley, unknown to other men, and it was worked by—Strangers, who were safe in that one small valley so long as they served the lord Vladimir, while anywhere else in the world all men would kill them."

"Why?" demanded Cunningham fiercely.

Stephan did not answer directly.

"I went down from the mountains that I loved, away from all my kin, and I went to the Governor of Daghestan and said that I wished to work in the mine of his son. And he sent me to a place, closely guarded, where there were others who were—as I was. And a long time later a boat came, and it took us many days upon the sea, and landed us secretly by night, and we traveled secretly, hiding, for many more days. And we came to the hidden valley ruled by the lord Vladimir and found two hundred other Strangers turned to slaves and working in the gold-mine he had discovered. They told us we would have done better to be stoned in our own villages than to come. We were driven to work with whips. If we rebelled we were shot down by the guards, who carried guns."

Gray moved suddenly.

"This was twenty years ago?" he demanded. "And you were kept a prisoner in that valley all that time, by guards with guns?"

"All of us," said Stephan quietly. He thrust with his foot at the body of Vladimir, lying in the dust before him. "That was our master. He had us taught the English language so that if other people came upon the valley we would seem to be of this nation. Three times—no, four times—wandering men came into the valley. None of them ever left it. They were killed by the guards...."

Gray stirred, his eyes moving fascinatedly from one to another of the Strange People.

"But we had been free men, once," said Stephan proudly. "We wept at first because we were—Strangers. Then we grew ready to fight because we were men. Many times, in those twenty years, we planned revolt. There were two or three Strangers among us who were from this nation. One of them became my wife and the mother of Maria. She had been a teacher in the schools, and she taught us much. But Vladimir seemed to hear our secret thoughts. Every time he forestalled our plans and punished us horribly for daring to think of revolt. Men said that he stretched threads of metal to our houses and that our words traveled to him along those threads, so that he knew always what we planned."

"Telephones," said Gray, fascinated, "but in the walls. Of course he could listen in."

"So at last we made our plans in the woods of the valley." Stephan spread out his hands. "We stole of the gold we dug. We gave it to five of our number, and they fled away. They bought horses and food—many horses and much food. They found a hiding-place for us. And while they were doing that, Vladimir was torturing us to learn where they had gone and why. But though four men and a woman died, they did not tell. And suddenly, in a night, we Strangers who were slaves of Vladimir, we fled from the valley. We killed the guards with our knives and vanished, hiding in the secret place the first five men had found. It was secret and secure. And then——"

Stephan hesitated.

"My wife, who was of this nation, had been born in these hills here. She told us of these hills as of Paradise. So we sent again a few of our number here. With the gold we had brought away, we bought ground. Then, a little by a little, all of us came. We kept far from other people. We did them no harm. Now they want to kill us, because Vladimir doubtless told them before he died that we were lepers, and because we are lepers, we must die."

He turned grimly to Cunningham and bared his forearm. And the skin of that forearm was silvery.

Cunningham's tongue would not move. Gray shivered.

"I'll—I'll admit," he said shakenly, "I didn't bargain for this. Good God!" He stared at the somber-faced Strangers with a queer terror. Then he shook himself suddenly. "But look here——!"

Cunningham found himself speaking hoarsely. "Not Maria!" he gasped. "Not Maria!"

Stephan's face, the color of ashes, had only compassion upon it as he watched Cunningham.

"Wait a bit," cried Gray. "Wait a bit! Stephan! That—that thing on your arm. It comes first on the elbows and knees, where the clothing rubs! Redness first, then this?"

"That is it," said Stephan quietly. "We have seen our children appear so. We have tried—ah, how we have tried!—to keep them from being Strangers too. But it is in the blood. Maria has showed it not even yet. But in time to come——"

"Nobody," panted Gray excitedly, "ever got it over fifty years of age!"

"Those who have come to us," said Stephan, "have always been young."

Gray struck his hands together.

"But it shouldn't be that way!" he cried. "It should take all ages. It should show on the face and hands! Not one of you shows it on the face or hands. There should be a dark band across the forehead. The fingertips should be silver, and the fingers should be twisted and bent. . . . Have you ever seen a doctor?"

Stephan smiled grimly. "That"—he pointed again to Vladimir's body—"when that was our master, he had a doctor to keep us alive. And there was never any doubt."

"I was at Ellis Island," said Gray excitedly. "I know what I'm talking——"

"It is finished," said Stephan grimly. "We die. Go and send your soldiers or your people to kill us."

"Cunningham, make him listen——"

"Go on, Gray," said Cunningham hoarsely. His face was ashen. "They'd only put us in some—some horrible colony somewhere. I—I don't want to live after this. If they want to die, let them. I'm going to stay and—and get killed with them, if I can."

"Idiot!" snapped Gray. "I've been telling you for half an hour that the symptoms are all wrong. And I was on Ellis Island and I know what they have got! And I know how they got it. Why, you idiot, don't you see that Vladimir was getting his father to send him slaves to work that damned mine? That the only way they could be kept as slaves would be to make them think they'd be killed if anybody else knew what he knew about them? They didn't get that thing naturally. They were deliberately inoculated with *psoriasis*, a sub-tropical skin affection that looks enough like leprosy to give anybody a start, but doesn't make a person unfit to work! These poor devils thought they were lepers, and they had a skin affection that is about as serious as dandruff! Creosote ointment or arsenic taken internally will cure it in ten days, and without one of those two things it lasts for years. Cooped up as they were, they reinfected each other. Believing themselves pariahs, they were afraid to run away from Vladimir until they had to. And he was trying to bluff them back to work in his mine. Don't you see, you idiot? Don't you see? It was a trick to get workers for his mine, workers who wouldn't dare be disloyal to him. And when they had run away, why, he had to get them back or they might find out themselves what he'd done and tell where his mine was and about all the crimes he's committed these twenty years back. Don't you see, Cunningham, don't you see?"

He turned to Stephan, who was staring at him incredulously.

"If you don't think I'm telling the truth," he snapped, "I'll go and kiss every pretty girl in camp to prove it! You've been here twenty years. I can't touch you. I can't deport you. And I'm mighty glad of it! As for killing Vladimir and his brother, I'm going to do my best to get you medals for the performance. I'm going to set my men on these fool farmers and chase 'em home. We'll sue them for the houses they've burnt. We'll put that sheriff in jail. We'll—we'll—— Cunningham, you lucky son-of-a-gun, I'm going to be best man and kiss the bride!"

But Cunningham was already preceding him in that occupation.

18

It was a very, very long time later. Cunningham was sitting peacefully upon the veranda of a house among tall mountains. His eyes roved the length of a valley that was closed in at the farther end by precipitous cliffs. There were small, contented sounds from the house behind him.

A motor-car rolled up a smooth, graded roadway. A man by the road saw the occupant of the car and shouted a greeting. Cunningham sprang to his feet and ran down to meet it.

Gray tumbled out of the car and gripped Cunningham's hand.

"I brought my fishing-rods," he announced exuberantly. "Where's that stream you were writing about?"

"Find it in the morning," said Cunningham happily. "How d'you like our valley?"

Gray came up the steps and stared out at the empty space below him. There were tall buildings down in the valley floor—great concrete buildings, with a tall shaft-house where motors whirred and an engine puffed.

"There ain't any such place!" announced Gray firmly. "I'm dreaming it! I found a concrete road leading here. I passed half a dozen motor-trucks on the way. And one scoundrel waved at me from a steering-wheel and I'll swear he's the chap that had a knife in the small of my back once, ready to stick it in."

"Quite likely," admitted Cunningham, grinning. "He is quite glad, now, that he did not stick it in. I've spread the news that you were the one who proved their title to the valley, through twenty years' occupation."

Gray squirmed, then grinned.

"Might be useful," he admitted, "to be popular here, in case there are any more fire-ceremonies going on."

Cunningham's face was serious for a moment.

"They were desperate, then," he said. "They'd tried the Christian God and things still looked black. So they called upon some ancient deities that their forefathers had worshiped.... You mustn't blame them, Gray."

"I don't." Gray grinned. "But I do want to study their dialect, Cunningham."

"Go ahead. It's disappearing. We're going in for politics, and boy scouts, and radios. We are a long way from a railroad, but our mine has built a road to it, and we have a motor-truck line that's as good as a trolley any day. We're highly civilized now, Gray."

He opened the door into the house. And there was Maria to smile and give Gray her hand.

"Your husband," said Gray, "has been boasting outrageously about what's happened in the valley since you people came back."

"He did it all," said Maria proudly. "Nobody does anything, ever, without asking him."

Gray chuckled and lifted an eyebrow at Cunningham.

"You haven't seen the prize exhibit yet," said Cunningham hastily. "Chief!"

There was a movement and Stephan came up a flight of steps that led outside. There was a tiny figure balanced on his shoulders. Stephan twinkled as he saw Gray, and he set his burden on the ground.

"I found him," he announced proudly, "going down the hillside with his air-rifle. He was going to hunt bears. That is a grandson!"

Gray stooped and beckoned. The small figure came shyly forward.

"Son," said Gray gravely, "don't you waste your time on small game like bears. Wait until you grow up a bit, and see a picture of a pretty girl in a magazine, and you find out where she is. And then—why, then you can start out on the route to romance and adventure."

[THE END]

Milton Keynes UK
Ingram Content Group UK Ltd.
UKHW030955261124
451585UK00005B/730